TRAIN ROBBERS OF MARS

KIT KANE

Published worldwide
by
Seven Monsters Media Ltd.

Cover Design by MiblArt
miblart.com

Cannonball Express logo by John Barrie

All Media Rights Enquiries:
Micheline Steinberg Associates
info@steinplays.com

ISBN: 978-1-9998750-7-7 (Hardcover)
ISBN: 978-1-9998750-3-9 (Paperback)

For Dulcie

Contents

1

Deathbed

"Please, Sara. I got a family. Three kids. You *know* that."

Sara Winchester *did* know that. Of course she did. One of those kids was pals with her own little Mikey. The youngest of the three could barely have been off the breast. This was a goddamn *family* Sara was swinging her merry old wrecking ball at here. A family she'd known—a family she'd *cared* about—for close on six years.

And yet, what else was she supposed to do?

Looking across her invoice-strewn desk—a soul-crushing paper landscape of pale red final reminders—Sara allowed herself one more unhappy moment to regard the man who stood opposite—the anguish in his eyes, the sagging shoulders beneath his dusty overalls, the palms of his leather-skinned laborer's hands turned towards her in a gesture almost of supplication. And even as Sara's heart sank further still, her mind continued with its feeble justifications: Deke Jones was young and fit; a solid, reliable worker; his chances of finding other employment had to be pretty good, right? *Right?*

All around, the peeling walls of Sara's rickety, pre-fab office unit seemed to close in, the sickly trickle of Martian light that managed to filter its way through the grimy windows seeming to deepen rather than alleviate the gathering gloom. From outside, the thud and grind of ongoing work in the adjacent yard drilled at Sara's temples...

Drawing in a deep breath, Sara unclenched her fists and finally met the eyes of the man standing before her. Met them with what she hoped was frankness and honesty. She owed the guy that at least. "Deke," she said, "I *swear* this is temporary. I've told everyone else the same. Soon as things turn around, you're back. *All* of you. You have my word. It's just that right now——"

"Dammit, Sara, we can barely pay our air tax as it is. How the hell are we gonna——"

"I understand. I *do*. And there *is* a small hardship fund available if——"

"Don't do this. Please, Sara, I'm begging you here. Don't do this."

But she did it anyway. Just as she had done with so many others this last disastrous year. Did it with the swiftness and suddenness you might use to put down a beloved pet. Whether that was to make things easier for her or for him, who the hell knew? Either way, fewer than ten seconds later, Deke Jones turned on his bootheels to go storming out of Sara's office, cursing with every furious footfall as he shouldered his way on past a small, silent figure lurking just beyond the doorframe on the step outside.

Hoping with all her heart that this second visitor might read the room and select a more appropriate moment to reveal the news they had clearly come to impart, Sara put her elbows on her desk, let her head drop into her hands, and issued a soul-weary sigh.

But no, apparently this particular news could not wait, and one tentative *ahem* later, Sara looked up again to take in the slight, singular figure of Doctor Isaac Lovelight. Perennially out of place in this bluest of blue collar environments—neat three-piece suit, floral necktie, shoes that glistened like two particularly fastidious beetles— the tiny man stood poised in the doorway, peering at Sara through fine, gold-rimmed spectacles, the black leather bag of his profession dangling from his perfectly manicured right hand.

Sara sighed again. "Not a good time, Isaac. *Really* not a good time."

"Oh, my love, it never is for the kind of news I come bearing."

An anguished groan heaved its way up from Sara's leaden gut, and moments later, she was accompanying the medical man through the company's dusty yard, heading reluctantly for Maintenance One. The vast building—biggest by far in the entire complex—loomed taller and more ominous with every step Sara took towards it, figuratively mirroring both her mounting problems and her spiraling anxiety. "So you're telling me it's just gonna get *worse?*" she said to Isaac as they tramped on through the yard, both of them careful to keep their voices low, lest they be overheard by any of the remaining workforce.

"Sara, he is *acutely* undernourished," Isaac replied. "When was the last time he even ate?"

Guilt clawed at Sara's gut. "You don't wanna know."

"Well... you *need* to get him back onto emergency fluids. And pronto."

"You think I don't *know* that?" and once again, the guilt dug in, ripping at Sara's insides like a tiger at the kill. "We're all out, Isaac. Done. Insurance won't cover it anymore. Insurance won't cover *anything* anymore."

Arriving at Maintenance One, Sara paused with Isaac by the building's main entrance, next to which, parked by itself in a muddy, oil-clogged bay, was Isaac's pickup—cleaner and more meticulously maintained than any working pickup had a right to be on this part of the Martian frontier. Much like its owner, many would hold.

"Sara, my love," the man said, and when he turned to her, the look in his eyes was as grave as Sara had ever seen in the pixie-like specimen that was Isaac Lovelight, "this breaks my heart, it truly does, but I have to be honest here. His entire body is failing. Failing *fast*. You *need* to understand that."

Sara opened her mouth to offer whatever pitiful excuse might emerge this time round, but the little man plowed on before anything could:

"If you do not get at least *some* essential nutrients into him soon," and graver still, Isaac hauled open the door to Maintenance One, a harsh, rusty creak echoing in the cavernous space beyond, "I promise you, losing a tooth is going to be the *least* of his concerns."

With these final words, Isaac's gaze shifted to the single titanic object that filled the flatbed of his pickup. Shifted, in fact, to the 'tooth' in question—its bloody, decayed root like the stump of some gigantic tree; the dental enamel of its massive, three-meter-tall business end glinting in the afternoon sun. At the same moment, almost as if on cue, a monstrous, rumbling roar rolled out through the open door of Maintenance One, the entire yard and its surrounding complex shaking from the sheer, gut-wrenching depth of sound. The effect was like being caught in a minor earthquake, and for several long seconds Sara watched Isaac's pickup tremble on its suspension, the business logo stenciled onto the truck's side— LOVELIGHT'S VETERINARY SERVICES— leaping and blurring before her eyes.

Eventually, once the roar had died away, Sara pulled in a slow, deep breath, turned to the open door of Maintenance One, and forced herself to step through it with Isaac. Step through it into a world filled with pain and hunger and the imminent death of everything Sara held dear.

2

Loading Up

What the hell was it with guys? Jess Flint thought. *Seriously, world! What?* And it wasn't the first time Jess had pondered this question today either. Truth be told, she'd found herself considering the matter all too frequently of late, arriving invariably at the conclusion that if guys were more like engines, the universe would be a far less confusing place. See, if an engine wasn't responding as per factory specs, you just stuck it on the bench, ran some diagnostics, and then tweaked that sucker till it did. Either that or got yourself a new damn engine. But if a *guy* wasn't responding as per... well, okay, sure, as analogies went, shaky ground perhaps. Point was though, if somehow there *had* been a factory producing guys, that place had some *serious* quality control issues. Cos as far as Jess could make out, *none* of their product *ever* responded quite as a final user might reasonably expect. Not once. And not least the example currently occupying the Cannonball Express's rearmost freight car with Jess.

Declan Donavan.

Oh, sure, the luxury model, no question, with all the fixtures and fittings a gal could possibly desire (not that Jess would ever claim a wealth of experience in such matters). But did the guy *like* her; *there* was the pertinent issue. Early indications had been positive, and yet, for reasons still to be ascertained, nothing so far had come of those indications. No actual romantic liaison of any kind arranged. And why? Who knew! Frankly, if that notional guy factory had had itself a notional complaints department, it would by now have been in receipt of the very stiffest of notional letters from one J. Flint (Dissatisfied of Tranquility).

A voice from outside the freight car interrupted Jess's frustrated musings:

"Okay, gang, last lot," and with a clomp and a clatter and a hiss-hiss-clunk, Sally Chu stepped up, strapped into the pilot's seat of her beloved steam-loader exoskeleton. Maneuvering the hulking robot suit up to the freight car's open side door, Jess's founding partner in Trans-Mars Haulage grinned her pin-up gal grin and set down the laden pallet in the steam-loader's arms. As the pallet's timber base hit the concrete floor outside the car, the stack of steel drums on it rattled and clanged together, their stark red warning labels—DANGER! URANIUM OXIDE - HIGHLY TOXIC!—dancing in the low evening sun that bathed the chemical refinery's loading yard.

"Dave!" Sally called out, and even before the rattle of the drums had died away, the fella so named came swooping in—Dave Hart, Jess's *other* founding partner in western Mars's most up and coming rail haulage company. With a speed and agility that belied his soft physique and less than heroic stature, TMH's 'temporal stowaway' from a twenty-first century Earth cut the plastic ties that held the drums to the pallet and took a step back.

"Much obliged," Sally said, before reaching out with one steam-powered robo-arm to lift the drum nearest her and pass it through the freight car's open door. "Comin' at ya," the gal announced, depositing the drum at the feet of Jess and Declan while Dave hopped nimbly on up into the same wagon to help with what was now the last of the evening's stowage duties.

One by one, the other drums followed, Jess, Declan, and Dave securing them to the freight car's interior with a network of webbing straps. As the three of them got into a steady work rhythm, Jess took the opportunity to make some further discreet study of the preposterously good-looking Irish fella beside her—the fella who may (or may not [or *may*]) in fact be attracted to her. Or not. The short term goal here, Jess had decided, would be to create an opening for one of them at least—maybe Declan, maybe Jess herself—to make some kind of positive move re the aforementioned but still largely theoretical romantic liaison thingy. And it was with this strategy in mind that Jess resumed her not-so-idle banter:

"Seriously?" she said. "How can you never have seen *The General*? Best movie *ever*."

"Really?" Declan replied, shaking his blonde fringe out of his eyes as he yanked tight one of the webbing straps. "I *have* sort of heard of it, if that's any consolation. Me, I'm more of a Douglas Fairbanks guy."

"Figures."

"Meaning?"

"Meaning *you* need to see more movies."

"Fair enough. So let me know next time this *General* is on at your local fleapit then."

Ha! Result! and Jess turned away to hide the involuntary smile that flitted across her face. "Okay, sure. I'll keep an eye on—"

"Which would be tomorrow night."

Uh-oh. Jess stiffened. *Busted.* "Um... what?" she managed. "Really? No *way!*"

"And which *you,* apparently, were entirely unaware of," Declan added, the smile that flitted across *his* face not even *slightly* involuntary.

"Well... I... I *was,*" Jess came back. "*Entirely* unaware, as you so rightly say."

"Despite the copious posters plastered all over Tranquility? Weird..." and damn damn *damn* that playful twinkle in the SOB's *gorgeous* frickin eyes...

"Okay, look," Jess said, "if you've got other stuff on tomorrow night, not a problem."

"Never said I had other stuff on."

"As did I. Not. Say."

"What?"

"God, I don't know... Look, forget I even mentioned it, okay? Just——"

"Oh, for the love of Betsy," came a frustrated growl from outside the freight car, and reaching through its open door with two robo-arms, Sally grabbed Jess and Declan by the backs of their overalls——one in each titanium fist——and hauled them both out of the wagon to let them dangle before her, their two pairs of workbooted feet pedaling in mid-air above the refinery's concrete floor.

"*You,*" Sally said to Declan with a take-no-shishkebab scowl, "pick her up at seven on the dot, and do *not* be late. And *you*..." she turned to Jess now, her scowl, if anything, even *less* tolerant of the cuss-word substitute, "wear a *frock,* and keep him waiting at least half an hour. More if he looks too cocky." A pause as Sally frowned then returned her attention to Declan. "And *you* did not hear that last bit," she said, before directing her concluding remarks to them both: "So... are we *clear* now? A nod will suffice."

Jess gulped then nodded, relieved to see Declan, still dangling beside her, do the same.

And with matters thusly settled, Sally jerked out a satisfied nod of her own then lowered Jess and Declan to the ground. "Okay, *good.* Now——"

But apparently, any further orders from Ms. Chu would have to wait, because just then a voice from behind cut in:

"Excuse me," it said, and turning with the others, Jess found herself looking up at an imposing middle-aged woman, chisel-featured, broad of shoulder, and dressed in overalls that were almost as dusty as Jess's.

"Hi," Jess said. "Can we help you?"

"I hope so," the woman replied, clearing her throat a little before turning to Declan. "I've been told that *you* are the buyer of this particular load, yes?" and she gestured to the train of eleven freight cars hitched behind the Cannonball in the

12

refinery's loading yard.

"Well, the organization I work for is the *actual* buyer," Declan said, "but I'm overseeing the purchase and transport, yes. Is there a problem?"

The woman shook her head. "No. No problem. It's just..." and she cleared her throat a second time. "I wonder if you might consider selling the shipment on."

Declan frowned. "Selling it *on?* To whom?"

"To me."

"I'm sorry, no can do. In case you haven't heard, this is the last high-grade Uranium 'O' in the sector. No more for at least a month now, or so the refinery bosses keep telling me."

The woman nodded, and though her attitude remained cool and businesslike, her eyes betrayed something else to Jess then—some underlying anxiety, some unspoken sense of urgency...

"Which is exactly my problem," the stranger continued, "and which is why I am willing to offer you twice market value for it."

Declan's own eyes widened. "Ah... well... tempting, to be sure. *Very* tempting. But again, no can do, I'm afraid. Our needs are——"

"*Three* times."

"... *Three* times market value? Are you *serious?*"

"In cash. Right now."

Declan stared back at the woman, who stood her ground in silence, awaiting a reply. In the end though, the Irishman shook his head. "That *is* a very generous offer, no question, but I'm sorry. Guess you'll have to wait till the month's out."

For a second, Jess thought she saw anger flare behind those troubled eyes, and the woman opened her mouth as if to say more... but then shut it again and nodded, her business here concluded it would seem, if not to her satisfaction. Following a final curt dip of the chin to Jess and the others, the woman turned on her bootheels and marched off, heading for the only non-rail vehicle parked in that section of the loading yard—a bubblegum pink and unfeasibly clean pickup truck, on the side of which were stenciled the words LOVELIGHT'S VETERINARY SERVICES. Waiting by the pickup was a small, neatly attired and bespectacled man, who, upon noting the woman's approach, opened the truck's driver's side door and settled himself in behind the wheel.

Along with Declan and the others, Jess watched in puzzled silence as the woman climbed into the pickup's passenger seat, following which the little man cranked the ignition, shifted the gearstick, and the truck trundled off in a cloud of rising dust.

"Hmmm," Jess said, arching a single eyebrow at Declan. "That was some serious profit you just turned down, fella."

Declan nodded. "Sure. But hey, gotta keep my

focus here, right? Cos with this little lot," and turning, he banged on the freight car they stood beside, his eyes sparkling with excitement as they took in the drums of uranium oxide that filled it, "we can *finally* bring New Avalon's reactors online. And that, folks, is one *seriously* big deal."

It was too, Jess had no doubt. Indeed, as far as 'deals' went, the top secret project known as New Avalon was as big as they came. Created millennia ago by the ancient Martians, the astonishing underground eco-system had been bio-engineered from the ground up as a way to produce a surfeit of oxygen that could replenish the planet's dying atmosphere, and since the discovery of the site— in a ruined state and minus its long dead creators—by outlawed activist group Free Air, renovation of New Avalon had been the rebels' number one priority. Understandably so, Jess thought. Even with the little she still understood of its science, she could see that the project had the potential to revolutionize life for the red planet's millions of human colonists. And the potential to put out of business for good the ruthless 'air barons' who ran so many of Mars's privatized air companies. According to Declan and his Free Air colleagues, once New Avalon was fully up and running again, and once it had been re-integrated with its network of sister sites, only one more of which had so far been discovered, it really would mean free air for all on Mars. That said, there was still a *lot* of work to be done—*years* of it as far as Jess could see—so although originally designed to be an *organic* system, if adding some temporary nuclear power into the mix hastened the process by which New Avalon could be brought back online, well then, all to the good in Jess's opinion.

"Believe me," Declan continued, "those reactors are gonna provide us with some *serious* grunt. They'll supercharge our irrigation systems, maybe even—"

"Hey all!"

The voice—warm and melodic, with the rounded tones of a born-and-bred Brit—emerged from the fine-featured face of Vera Middleton, the fourth and final founding member of Trans-Mars Haulage, and the company's accountant/administrator/mistress-of-all-paperwork.

Notebook in hand, the English gal approached the waiting group at her usual efficient trot, peering at them over the rims of her 'Madame Librarian' eyeglasses.

"Hey girl," Jess said as her friend came to a stop beside them. "How'd you get on?"

"Not as well as I'd hoped," Vera replied, the most delicate of frowns creasing the gal's flawless alabaster brow. "The town *is* rather busy, and I could only get three rooms in total, so I'm afraid some of us *will* have to, you know, double up."

Never one to waste an opportunity as tease-worthy as the preceding, Sally, still towering over them in her steam-loader, unsheathed a wicked grin and waggled her eyebrows at Jess and Vera. "Well hey, you know me, gals. I'll 'double up' with most anyone. Feel free to draw straws," and, her loader mimicking her every move, Mars's foremost exponent of the showgirl shimmy did her foremost thing, before segueing into a cartoonish, sexy-cute pose, buttoning the entire cornball routine with a mischievous pout in Vera's direction.

In response to which, as was her unfailing custom, Vera gulped in deepest embarrassment and blushed like a ripening apple, looking anywhere but at the brazen hussy in the giant robot-suit. "Um, a-a-actually, Sally," the English gal stammered, "I've p-p-put *you* in with Jess. And I've given *me* the single room. Hope that's, um…" cue a further gulp "…okay…?"

As the sole person present who knew of Vera's intense crush on their own Ms. Chu, Jess smiled to herself and waited for Sally to pile in with further teasing… only to be surprised when the gal came back not with more of the same but with what appeared to be a disgruntled frown, her steam-loader sagging around her and magnifying a body language that looked for all the world like foot-shuffling awkwardness.

Hmmmm, Jess mused. *So* that *was a most un-Sally-like response. Most un-Sally-like indeed.* What on earth had been going through the gal's head just then?

3

Twin Room Torment

"She *hates* me," Sally Chu said, directing her statement at the half-open door of the hotel room's en suite. "In every possible way a gal can hate, that gal frickin hates *me*."

"Vera does *not* hate you, Sal," came Jess's weary reply, drifting through from the en suite to the bedroom and prompting in Sally a huff of frustration. It was not, by a *long* chalk, the first time Sally had heard this idiotic rebuttal tonight, and in response to it now she proceeded to compose in her head several possible comebacks, few if any of which would find their way into *The Nice Girl's Guide to Appropriate Frickin Language*. In the end though, Sally buttoned her lip and just sagged back onto the upholstered headboard of her bed, where she huffed a bit more, hugged her knees, and stared out through the single window of the tiny hotel room. Not that the view there provided much comfort, consisting as it did of several rows of rickety rooftops, beyond which lay the chemical refinery the small township served, its perpetual glow warming the lower regions of an otherwise pitch black Martian sky.

"I mean, look," Sally said eventually, "I get it, okay? She's a classy babe. Used to hob-nobbing with her classy English friends back on classy ol' Planet Earth…"

"Vera does *not* hate you, Sal," the voice of the idiot monopolizing the bathroom repeated.

"Yeah, right," Sally growled back, and rising with a frown, she stepped up to the room's full-length mirror to scowl at the young Asian woman framed in its mottled glass. "You seen what she's like. I go anywhere *near* that gal, I swear she thinks she's gonna catch something. Catch what exactly, I have no frickin clue." Sally scowled again at her image in the hotel room mirror. "Terminal *hotness,* maybe? Stage 3 *everyone-else-would-kill-for-this?*"

"You don't think maybe she just finds you a little… intimidating?"

Sally snorted. "Oh, please! *Me? Intimidating?* It's *her* that's got the frickin vowels that built an empire! And damned if she don't know *exactly* how to use 'em either. Do you know, she actually says the word 'golly'. For *real*. In *actual sentences*. Not even sure I ain't heard a 'jolly good' or two in there neither. And it's *me* that's intimidating? Ha!"

In response to which entirely irrefutable arguments, the bathroom-hogger next door proceeded only to compound her idiocy: "So why do you even care?"

"*Care?*" Sally exclaimed. And hey, if more snorting accompanied the exclamation, who the hell could blame a gal, right? "What do you mean, *care?* I don't *care.*" And she didn't. Of *course* she didn't. Had the serious *hots* for? Yeah, sure. Would dearly love to ride the bedsprings with? Darn tootin', mon ami! Vera 'Drop Dead English' Middleton was just about the single most desirable human Sally Chu had ever met, regardless of the fact that the lady herself clearly had no clue about this. No clue whatsoever. Gal *smelled* amazing too. Like, *all the time,* in a way that seemed to defy the very laws of biology. But *care?* Ha! Time to clarify the hell outta that little misunderstanding:

"Seriously, babe," Sally continued to Jess through the half-open door of the en suite, lacing her throaty drawl with what she hoped was just the right edge of withering derision, "do I *look* like I *care* what Vera Middleton thinks of me?"

"Um… well you sure *sound* like you——"

"It's the *principle,* babe. The frickin *principle.* Me? I take people as they are. Always have done, always will. But her? Oh no. You seen the way she looks at me, right? Or, more to the point, *doesn't* look at me. Like, *ever.* Nope. To her, I am just a Grade A tramp, yeah? Trash. *Trampash,* that's what I am. A hussy. A frickin *trampashussy,* that's ol' Sally Chu."

A sigh from Her Next Door. "If you say so…"

"I mean, look, can I help it if I got natural assets?" and here Sally shot a careless look at her own cleavage in the mirror. "Proud of 'em too. Always have been. Always will. Ain't never changed for no one, me, and I sure as hell ain't starting now," following which impassioned assertion, Sally proceeded to lace up the gaping neckline of her black satin babydoll, adopt what she imagined to be a slightly less T&A posture, and study the overall effect in the mirror…

… before rolling her eyes and succumbing to a frustrated half-snarl. *Dammit,* what the hell was she *doing?* and turning to glare again at the half-open door of the en suite, Sally snapped out a tetchy, "Look, are you about done in there, hon?"

"Um… nearly," came Jess's reply.

"What the hell ya even up to anyway?"

"Oh, um, nothing. Don't come in though."

Huh? Sally thought. *Don't come in?* Okay, so *this* had just become moderately interesting—not to say a welcome distraction from troubling self-scrutiny—and stepping away from the mirror, Sally strode towards the en suite, shoved its door fully open, and barged on through into the brightness of the lamplit bathroom.

"Hey! I *said* don't come *in!*" a startled Jess yelped, her head whipping round to fire a furious glare at Sally—

—who, in turn, froze where she stood in the doorway, mouth hanging open as she took in the spectacle presented by her seated friend.

"Girl, if you so much as smile," Jess growled, "I swear I will kick your hottie ass."

As hilariously unlikely as the outcome just proposed might have been, it was, Sally felt, nowhere *near* as unlikely as the sight of the gal who had proposed it.

Perched on the bathroom's lone stool, Jess Flint sat before the washstand mirror, eyeliner pencil in one hand, sundry other makeup offerings arrayed before her, engaged, Sally was forced to assume, in some puzzling effort at cosmetic enhancement. *Puzzling* because, well, the actual *results* of that effort were... Fighting back the torrent of quips that begged to be released to a deserving world, Sally instead enquired with as much straight-faced sincerity as she could muster:

"Um... care to explain, babe?"

For a moment, only that scorch-the-flesh-from-your-bones glower continued to communicate the simmering emotions of Jessica Ashley Flint. But then, eventually: "I... I got this stuff at the drugstore in town."

"... Uh-huh..."

"Thought I'd, you know, maybe try some of it out..."

"... Uh-huh..."

More glowering, more simmering, until finally, Jess threw the eye pencil onto the ledge beneath the mirror, screeched her stool back half a meter, and turned her glare up to *incinerate*. "Okay, look, thanks to *your* big goddamn mouth, I have now got a big goddamn date tomorrow night."

"And you are most goddamn welcome. *And...?*"

"*And...* maybe I oughtta, you know, make some kinda effort, or something, right? *Right?*"

"Well, sure... and that effort would involve impersonating a victim of serious assault *why?*" Yeah, okay, cheap shot, but honestly, how else was Sally supposed to react here? The gal before her truly did look like she'd just gone ten rounds with... well, with *Sally*.

Glare ripening still further, Jess snatched a tissue from the box on the washstand and scrubbed angrily at the almost childlike attempts she'd made to augment her eyes. Unfortunately, the move succeeded only in smudging those attempts even more. "*Dammit!*" Jess spat, throwing the now empty tissue box at a nearby waste basket and rising to barge her way past Sally in the bathroom doorway. "Dammit dammit *dammit,*" she repeated, those panda-in-a-punch-up eyes of hers lasering in on a fresh box of tissues that sat on the table beneath the window.

"Seriously, babe," Sally said as she tailed her furious roomie, "it's like you never picked up an eye pencil in your entire life."

What followed this harsh but inarguable observation was silence. A whole heap of it.

"Oh my *god!*" Sally blurted. "You never picked up an eye pencil in your entire life!"

Ripping open the fresh box of tissues, Jess whirled on Sally. "Oh, come *on,* Sal! It's *me!* When would *I* ever need to use makeup? Most times, it's all I can do to get the axle grease outta my hair every night. Not like I even—" at which point, completely without warning, Jess stopped— stopped *dead*—her gaze directed out the bedroom window, her eyes widening. "What the *hell...?*"

Sally frowned. "Huh? You okay, babe?" and moving in behind Jess, she too peered through the room's small, grimy window, though if she had been expecting enlightenment to follow, she was disappointed. Outside, in the distance, Sally could just make out a diesel locomotive with a long train of freight, trundling past on the mainline track beyond the chemical refinery. But apart from that, there was, as far as Sally could see, nothing else of note. Certainly nothing to justify Jess's apparent shock. "Babe, what is it? I don't know what you're—"

"First wagon," Jess said, and frowning deeper, Sally turned to look again at the distant freight train—this time at its first wagon.

That was when Sally's own eyes started in shock, her heart leaping at the same time.

The thing was, such had been the frantic, never-a-minute-to-spare nature of forming, promoting, and running Trans-Mars Haulage, Jess and her crew had so far gotten round to painting the company logo onto just *one* of their many freight cars. And now, framed in the hotel room window, there that very freight car was, its two-meter-tall, bright yellow TMH logo almost glowing in the dark behind the diesel locomotive the car was now hitched to. But that wasn't all. Not *nearly* all. Because *behind* that freight car were another ten— maybe not so readily identifiable as the first, but recognizable in context nonetheless.

"Holy crap!" Sally said. "That's our frickin cargo!"

4

Train Robbers of Mars

Whirling from the window, Jess flew across the hotel room floor, hauled open the door, and hurled herself through. Bare feet pounding threadbare carpet, she covered the length of the second-floor corridor in moments, hammering at two of the doors along it as she sprinted past.

"Downstairs now!" she yelled, barely slowing as she issued the command, let alone stopping to wait for an answer. "We got a problem!" and even as Jess came stumbling to a halt at the corridor's far end, she heard the two doors she'd hammered on clatter open behind her, followed by the bleary voices of first Vera then Declan:

"Golly, Jess, you *scared* me! What's going on?"

"Yeah, whassup?"

But Jess was already gone, dragging open the door at the end of the passage and pitching herself through it onto the landing atop the stairs. Fortunately, Sally was also on the case now, the gal's voice ringing out from behind Jess as she gave chase: "What the boss lady said! BIG problem!"

Tumbling down the single flight of stairs, Jess hit the hotel lobby in seconds, barged her way out through the building's front door, and skidded to a halt on the stoop, her fury surging as she spotted the receding diesel and its stolen cargo, still just visible in the distance, heading northwards out of town.

Exactly what Jess intended to *do* about any of this, though, remained, for the moment, a mystery, and as she stood there peering through the gloom of the Martian night, watching Declan's precious cargo disappear into the darkness, the best Jess could manage was an enraged growl followed by some Sally-grade cursing.

A heartbeat later, as if summoned by the profanity, the benchmark-for-cursing herself came tumbling out onto the hotel's stoop, black satin babydoll billowing in her wake. "Aw god*damn* it!" Sally spat as she and Jess watched the train's rearmost freight car vanish in the night. "What *now?*"

Jess spun to Sally and opened her mouth to reply, but before she could, the hotel's front doors crashed open for a third time, and Declan and Vera all but fell through them. Like Jess and Sal, both were clad only in their nightwear.

"Will somebody *please* tell me what the hell is going on here?" Declan demanded.

"We been robbed," Jess said. "They *took* it! *All* of it! Whole damn cargo!"

At this grim revelation, Jess fully expected Declan to go ballistic, but weirdly, that's not what happened. Instead, Jess watched a *different* kind of emotion—a sort of open-mouthed horror— transform the Irishman's features as the fella took in Jess herself. Principally, the parts of Jess located between her neck and her hairline.

"Oh my god!" Declan exclaimed. "Jess, what did they *do* to you? Are you okay?"

"Huh? What are you— Oh! No, that's not—" Jess made to swipe at the makeup smudges around her eyes, then thought better of it. "Um, see, that isn't actually—"

But before she could say more, Trans-Mars Haulage's final crew member came barging through the exit to join them on the stoop, huffing and puffing in his flannel nightshirt. "What is it?" Dave gasped. "What's going on?"

"We been robbed," Declan declared. "They beat Jess up."

Aaaaannnd now it was *Dave's* turn to recoil in horror as he too took in Jess's face:

"Oh god, Jess, are you okay?"

"Yes! *Yes,* I'm *fine! Really!* It's not what you—"

"Bloody scumbags! I'll go get a first-aid kit."

"Guys, guys, *relax,*" Sally said. "They did *not* beat Jess up, okay? That's actually just—"

"OIL!" Jess blurted. "Or... *something...*"

Vera frowned. "Um... *really?* You don't *wash* before you put your *pajamas* on?"

"Look, can we maybe discuss this later? Cos in case y'all haven't noticed—" Jess jabbed a somewhat irate finger in the direction of the distant railroad. "Train robbery! We gotta follow 'em! Don't know how, but—"

"Babe..." It was Sally's voice—low, thoughtful, and tinged (as it so often was in times of crisis) with the kind of *chill-folks-we-got-this* attitude that made Jess love the gal like a sister.

Grabbing Jess by the shoulder, Sally whirled them both around to face the opposite end of the hotel's stoop, fixed to which, Jess saw, there was a sturdy timber rail. And hitched to that rail? Several similarly sturdy horses, slurping at a drinking trough.

Jess turned again to Sally, and the look in the gal's eye said all that needed to be said.

5

Dress Down Fridays

Leaving the others agape and standing, Jess and
Sally launched themselves for the far end of the
stoop, vaulting the rail there to land by a pair of
towering stallions, one chestnut, one a dappled
gray. Unprepared for the impact as the soles of her
bare feet slammed into gravelly ground, Jess
stifled a cry of pain, then grabbed the reins of the
dappled gray and hoisted herself into the saddle,
slotting her traumatized feet into stirrups she
could barely reach but which would just have to
do. Beside her, Sally was already thrusting her
heels into the flanks of her own ride, and as the
gal's chestnut stallion took off, Jess kicked the

dappled gray into action too, the animal surging forward after Sal's.

Jess's horse was powerful, responsive, and, crucially, *fast*. Within seconds she had drawn level with Sally, the pair of them thundering along after the diesel and its stolen cargo, visible once more up ahead. Which meant, of course, that they were catching the train up. Though maybe not for long, Jess thought. Currently negotiating a tight bend on its way out of town, the loco would surely accelerate once it hit any significant straight, and after that, the chances of outrunning it on horseback would diminish rapidly to zero.

Not gonna happen, Jess assured herself and dug her heels deeper into her galloping mount.

Beside Jess, over the thudding of hooves and the rumble of the train ahead, Sally's voice suddenly rang out in a wild, exultant whooping, and when Jess shot a startled look at her friend, she saw the beaming gal run a wry gaze over Jess's flapping pajamas, before looking down at her own wind-buffeted babydoll. "Gotta love these dress-down Fridays, huh?"

Jess grinned right back. "Hell yeah!" she said, and then, "HYAH!" as once again she kicked her heels into the dappled gray's flanks, the animal surging forward in tandem with Sal's.

Fewer than ten seconds later, they had closed the distance between them and the train to just meters, galloping on into the dense dust storm wake that billowed behind the thundering rolling stock. One final bare-heeled spurring was all it took, and at last, hoofbeats pounding their relentless tattoo, Jess and Sally's horses drew level with the train's rearmost wagon.

Even before Jess could yell "What now?" Sally rose on her stirrups and launched herself from her saddle, sailing through the dust-filled air. Jess gasped in both shock and disbelief, but she needn't have worried; Sally landed neatly on the narrow railed-off ledge at the very back of the last wagon, hauling herself up to safety as her now riderless chestnut stallion dropped back, vanishing into the night behind them.

Damn, but that gal made it look sooooo easy...

Heart hammering, Jess maneuvered her own horse into the position Sally's ride had just vacated—level with and just meters from the train's rearmost freight car. This close up, the clatter of wheels on track was almost deafening, and the train's churning dust cloud wake lashed at Jess's face, blinding her for seconds at a time.

Crouched less than three meters away on the narrow back ledge of the rear wagon, Sally beckoned furiously to Jess, yelling out, "Come on! You got it, girl!"

Yes, dammit, she *did.* Whoever the hell these train robbers were, they were *not* getting away with this. Not if Jessica Ashley Flint had anything to say on the matter.

Hoisting her left foot over the saddle so that both her legs were on the side facing the train, Jess peered through the dust storm at the speeding railcar her horse kept pace with. At the same time, her right foot remained locked in its stirrup, ready to give her the push off she would need for the leap. But with her straining fingers struggling to maintain their grip on the saddle behind her, just stopping herself being thrown from the jouncing horse was a challenge in itself. How the hell was she supposed to judge a jump like this when she could barely stay upright?

And then the train began to accelerate.

Gaze whipping front once more, Jess swore in frustration. Because, yes, as she'd feared, the diesel had just hit a long stretch of straight track and was taking full advantage, pulling away from Jess and her horse with startling speed.

"Do it!" Sally yelled over the thunder of the wheels. "You got this, babe! *Do* it!"

Jess sucked in a deep breath—*now or never*—and coiling her body like a spring, she shoved off from the stirrup, leaping for the rear ledge of the speeding freight car.

And could the enterprise have gone any worse? No, ma'am, it could not. Even as she launched herself into the chasm between galloping stallion and hurtling train, Jess felt her right foot slip *through* the stirrup it was using to push off from. Slip through and then catch on that same closed semicircle of hardened steel. While her body sailed onward for the wagon ahead, and her reaching hands grabbed the safety rail of its rear platform, Jess felt her right leg yanked up behind her, foot still caught fast in the stirrup.

And did the whole horrific fiasco end there? Not a chance. Because the train *continued* to pull away, and the dappled gray *continued* to drop back, and strung out like so much washing between accelerating train and retreating horse, Jess felt the stirrup bite into her bare ankle even as her fingers fought to retain their grip on the freight wagon's rear safety rail. "Oh god," Jess gasped, every vertebra in her spine stretching towards some inevitable breaking point, until finally, unable to maintain their hold any longer, Jess's pain-wracked fingers snapped free of the rail, and the front half of her body went plummeting towards the boulder-strewn ground rushing by beneath.

6

Heroes in PJs

Since the unanticipated founding of Trans-Mars Haulage earlier in the year, Jess Flint had come to reflect with surprising (not to say alarming) regularity that, these days, her life seemed to benefit from way more than its fair share of thank-the-sweet-lord-for-Sally-Chu moments.

And here, right on cue, came another one.

Lunging forward with panther-like speed, Sally thrust both hands over the safety rail at the back of the hurtling freight car and grabbed Jess's forearms, halting at once the deadly plunge that threatened to send Jess face first into the rushing, stony surface of the red planet. Not that death, imminent and bloody, ceased still to loom large. Slung like a hammock between galloping horse and speeding train—single stirrup holding her fast at one end, Sally (thank-the-sweet-lord-for) Chu gripping her at the other—Jess remained utterly helpless, unable to do anything but stare down in heart-thumping horror as, less than two meters beneath her, that jagged terrain of bone-shattering rock continued to race past at forty or more kph.

"It's okay, I gotcha," Sally yelled to Jess, but no sooner had the words left the gal's mouth than the horse attached to Jess's ankle began to drop back again, and the pain in Jess's wracked spine cranked its way up to excruciating once more.

Stifling a cry, Jess shook and twisted her foot to try and free it from the stirrup. But with no slack to speak of, the effort brought only further pain, and the stirrup's semicircle of hardened steel remained stuck where it was, caught just above Jess's ankle.

Then the dappled gray dropped back farther still, and this time there was no chance of stifling it—Jess screamed, a full-throated howl of agony.

In response, Sally's already vice-like grip on Jess's forearms tightened, and she heaved hard, yanking Jess towards her. But it was no use: the cold steel of the stirrup only bit deeper into Jess's ankle flesh, its straight-edged tread lodged fast behind her heel bone.

"No!" Jess yelled. "Gimme some slack! Now!"

"*Slack?* Are you *insane!*"

"NOW!" Jess screamed, and with a grim nod, Sally complied, allowing her hold to loosen and Jess's forearms to slip backwards through Sally's fingers. Just a little, the gal's formidable grip locking in again around Jess's wrists, but the result was at least *some* slack, and praying it would be enough, Jess once more jerked her foot in the stirrup.

Nothing.

She kicked out hard, one, twice, three times, foot flailing in the dusty air as Mars raced by a meter-and-a-half beneath her.

Still nothing.

Breath now coming in harsh, ragged gasps, and with despair closing in, Jess pulled her knee towards her, kicked out yet again, hauled inwards a second time—

—and bingo! Finally, her foot slipped free, the hard steel tread of the stirrup sliding past her heel and falling away as Jess's knee shot up towards her chest.

With Sal still clutching her by the wrists, Jess felt the rear half of her body drop like a sack of wet cement, legs plummeting for the rocky ground rushing by below. But at the very same instant, roaring her defiance, Sally hauled hard, pulling Jess towards the freight car. Tumbling over the low steel balustrade of the safety rail, Jess slammed into Sally's midriff, and together the pair of them went careering backwards onto the wagon's rear platform, thudding to a halt in a graceless heap of limbs, hair, pajama flannel, and torn black satin.

After a moment, Jess dragged herself into a sitting position so that her back lay flat against the freight car's sealed rear door, and for several seconds more, there she sat, huffing and gasping and trying hard not to contemplate all the ways in which what they had just done had been insane-to-the-point-of-suicidal.

Beside her, Sally simply brushed her hair out of her eyes and straightened her disheveled nightwear. "Know what?" she said. "Something tells me this is *not* conducive to a good night's beauty sleep."

With her breathing finally dropping back to levels that might *just* allow concurrent speech, Jess squinted into the dark behind the speeding train. "You see any of the others yet?"

Sally didn't even bother to look. "Are you serious?"

"I thought they'd be right behind us. There *were* other horses there, right?"

"Yeah, but ain't none of them can ride for beans, hon. Nope, they, bless their city-folk hearts, are gonna have to source themselves some alternative transportation."

●●●

Vera hauled open the driver's door of the ATV, glanced at the dash, and once again felt her heart sink. The diesel four-wheel-drive would surely have been ideal, but with no keys in the ignition, and no Jess or Sally to hotwire the thing, the vehicle, like the other examples Vera had just vetted, might as well have not been there at all.

Slamming the ATV's door in frustration, Vera turned from it and raced on through the darkened yard of the closed chemical refinery, scanning the gloom for any other potential rides and finding none. Maybe Declan was having better luck, she thought, but just seconds later, she rounded a corner to meet the fellow himself concluding his own search from the yard's other side, and the look on the Irishman's face told the same story.

"Well?" Vera asked anyway.

"Nothing," Declan said. "You?"

Vera shook her head, and together the pair of them took off once more across the shadow-drenched compound, skidding to a stop just moments later beside the steam-powered hulk of the Cannonball Express. Now hitched only to its coal tender, crew car, passenger car, and the empty flatbed for Sally's steam-loader, the gleaming red loco remained parked where they'd left it earlier that evening, untouched, it would seem, beyond the theft of its cargo. Apparently, the robbers had simply uncoupled said cargo from the Cannonball end then re-coupled it to their own diesel loco at the *other*, before making off with all eleven trucks, the entire heist conducted under the non-existent eyes of the refinery's non-existent security detail.

"Dave, please tell me you got this," Declan growled through gritted teeth.

Huddled over the controls in the cab of the Cannonball, a clench-jawed Dave yanked on a lever then twisted two valves simultaneously. Determined look and purposeful activity aside though, the fellow did not, Vera thought, present the aspect of a happy bunny.

"She'll be up to pressure in about an hour," Dave said. "Best I can do."

"*What?*" Declan shot back. "By which time they are gonna be god knows where. *Dammit!*"

"Okay, look," Vera said, "it's a railway, yes? How hard can it be to follow them? Not like they've got free rein to go anywhere they want, is it?"

Declan glowered at her, the beginnings of some angry objection rising in his eyes. But Vera was having none of that. Not with her friends' lives potentially relying on quick and decisive action here. "*You,*" she snapped at Declan, "get with the

41

shoveling," following which she whirled on Dave in the cab. "And *you,* vent the boiler to fifty percent capacity. That should get us up to pressure faster. Well what are you waiting for? Go go *go!*"

And almost instantly, the boys leapt to it, taking Vera momentarily by surprise. "Golly," she murmured to herself. "And they went went went…"

• • •

Huddled together on the narrow platform at the back of the speeding freight car, Jess and Sally hauled at the heavy steel door set into the car's rear end. With the pair of broad sliding panels on the wagon's flanks providing primary access for loading up, the smaller back door was essentially rusted shut through years of apparent non-use, and Jess and Sal's first two attempts to pull the thing open got them precisely nowhere. But then, after a third coordinated heave, the grimy rectangle of metal wrenched free of its corroded frame and swung aside in a swirling cloud of rust flakes.

Faint silver light from an unusually clear and starry Martian sky spilled into the dark interior of the freight car, and after a moment, as her eyes grew accustomed to the gloom, Jess began to make out the squat tubular shapes of the uranium ore drums—dozens of them, stacked three or four high, strapped to the walls and floor of the wagon.

With, as far as it was possible to tell, no black-hatted welcoming committee waiting there to whup their idiot asses, Jess and Sally exchanged looks of relief, and Sally darted through into the wagon itself to crouch low behind the nearest stack of drums.

Jess followed, ducking down beside her friend. "You think they saw us get on?"

Sally shrugged. "If they did, expect the merry thud of incoming bad guys any moment."

They waited... and heard nothing but the rhythmic clatter of wheels on track and the rush of wind past the sides of the wagon.

"I'm guessing *not* then," Sally said.

Jess rose to her feet, a righteous fury finally vanquishing the last of her fear. "Okay, so let's go take out these scumbags and get our damn—"

"Whoah whoah whoah, Douglas Fairbanks," Sally said, pulling Jess down again into their hiding place behind the drums. "Just dial back the action hero a notch, huh?"

Jess scowled at her friend. "What? *Why?*"

Sally, sensitive as ever, offered the mother of all patronizing eye-rolls before continuing: "One: we have no idea how many bad guys we're dealing with here. Two: we have no idea how heavily armed they are. And three: *we are in our pajamas.*"

All good points and well argued, Jess was forced to concede. "So what's the plan?"

"Okay," Sal said, "first up, there *is* still a chance that Dave, Vera, and Declan might swoop in with some sort of super heroic rescue bid involving heavy artillery, delightful banter, and the full might of Western Mars Law Enforcement."

"You think?"

"No, of course not. What am I, an idiot? But hey, you never know, right?"

"And if the others *don't* show?"

"If they *don't* show, well then, right now we have got ourselves the element of surprise, yeah? So let's not waste it. Reckon we lay low in here till the train gets to wherever it's going. Then, provided Lady Luck stays on our side, we wait till whatever crew there is up front clears outta the loco, following which we steal the whole damn shooting match back again, from right under their thieving scumbag noses."

Jess weighed this up. "Okay, nice," she said. "Laying low could be a problem though. What if somebody comes back to check on the cargo?"

For a moment, they pondered in silence, then Jess's gaze shifted to take in the stacked drums of uranium ore… before darting back to Sally, whose grinning mug revealed at once that great minds thought alike.

Just five minutes later, Jess and Sal had prized the lids off two of the steel drums, hauled those same drums out through the freight car's end door, and were emptying the drums' contents onto the single track railroad that unspooled behind the hurtling train...

7

End of the Line

Stifling a sigh of disappointment, Vera offered her thanks to the fellow she'd spent the last ten minutes questioning and took her leave of the signal box, stepping out from its lofty main cabin and onto the steeply descending access stairs of the tower it sat atop. At the foot of the tower, the complex rail junction of Mars West 30—the most elaborate in the entire region—lay spread out before Vera, a mind-boggling spaghetti of steel and timber lit by a low morning sun whose russet splendor did little to lift Vera's sunken spirits.

To be sure, the fellow manning the signal box had been as obliging as anyone could possibly be, his eagerness to help fueled by the same intense hatred of train robbers that burned in the veins of most Martian rail workers. But while the man had admitted to being on shift since early last night, he remained adamant that nothing fitting the description of the robbers' diesel had come through the junction at any point in the last nine hours.

Descending the signal box steps, Vera hit Martian dirt once more and began to make her way back to the siding where they'd left the Cannonball, the loco's dazzling red and brass livery ablaze in the early morning sunshine. Halfway there, she caught sight of Declan and Dave, the pair appearing almost simultaneously, on the way back from their own separate enquiries and each sporting a near identical frown of dissatisfaction.

"No luck then?" Vera asked as the three of them converged and then hurried on together for the Cannonball.

The two boys shook their heads.

"Which," Vera said, "would seem to confirm what the chap in the box says. Nothing like our robbers' train through all night."

"So we've lost 'em," Dave growled, tramping along at Vera's shoulder. "Great."

"No, we have *not* lost them," Vera replied. "All this means is that we have to use our brains. Make enquiries. Interview leads."

"Leads?" Dave said. "What leads? We ain't got no leads."

"Actually..." came Declan's voice from behind, and alerted by something in the musing tone of it, Vera paused mid-stride and turned to look over her shoulder at the Irishman.

Declan had stopped several meters back and stood peering at a rickety timber outbuilding on whose paneled front had been fixed a large cork noticeboard. Covering every square centimeter of the board's real estate was a dense clutter of paper—posters, leaflets, notices, all fluttering in the gentle morning breeze—and as Vera watched, Declan plucked one of the more colorful leaflets from the noticeboard's top left corner. From where she stood, Vera was unable to make out the leaflet's actual contents, but whatever they were, a moment's study of them brought to Declan's face something that *did* finally raise Vera's spirits. Something that looked to her very much like a thoughtful—even a *hopeful*—smile...

•••

Lady Luck was a bitch.

Such was the considered opinion of Jessica Ashley Flint, and on current evidence, it was an opinion unlikely to change anytime soon. Still huddled in the cramped and acrid-smelling darkness of her emptied ore drum, it seemed to Jess that she'd barely registered the robbers' train lurching to what turned out to be its final stop before she heard the clatter of the cargo wagon's doors opening, followed almost immediately by the sound of voices:

A male voice came first: "How many?"

Then a female: "Four barrels should do for now. Bring 'em all straight to the lab."

"Will do."

Great. Just great. Because they couldn't have chosen any of the *other* cargo wagons to unload *first* now, could they? Any of the *other* cargo wagons that *didn't* contain a couple of pajama-clad, deathwish-harboring, idiot stowaways? No, of course they couldn't.

As previously mentioned: bitch.

With her brain processing as best it could the noises that followed, Jess heard what sounded like two people clamber up into the wagon, then a series of rumbles, clanks, and clicks as the unseen pair presumably selected, unstrapped, and then extracted the four barrels the female voice had requested. The hydraulic hiss of what might have been some kind of forklift or steam-loader accompanied the sounds. Fully expecting her own barrel to be one of the four chosen, and with frankly no plan whatsoever to deal with said eventuality, Jess braced herself for the lurching

49

that would surely follow once the drum she was in was grabbed by the two individuals at work in the freight car. As it happened, however, Lady L appeared at this point *finally* to cut Jess a break, and several seconds later, the ongoing sounds of manual labor moved from *inside* the cargo wagon to *outside,* Jess's drum remaining happily in situ.

As those same sounds grew fainter still with distance, Jess risked a whisper:

"Sally? I think they've gone."

No answer.

"Sal?"

Still nothing.

Curled up in her ore drum like some kind of human snake-in-a-can, Jess pressed her upper back into the underside of the drum's lid, which she'd previously pulled down on top of her only just firmly enough to stop it rattling about in the course of the wagon's normal movement. With the mildest of upward shoves, the circle of steel duly popped off, Jess just managing to catch the thing before it clattered to the floor of the wagon.

As her head rose above the rim of the barrel, Jess was forced to squeeze her eyes shut for several seconds, the light streaming in through the freight car's open side door dazzling her after her time in the total darkness of the ore drum.

Ready to duck back down again at the slightest hint of trouble, Jess waited a moment in breathless silence, before finally uncoiling her cramped and aching body from the cylinder of metal and stepping out onto the floor of the wagon.

"Sally?" she whispered again but with the same result as before.

Glancing round, Jess noted that several of the webbing straps securing the other drums to the freight car's walls and floor had, as she had guessed, been unbuckled, and that a number of the drums (four, she presumed, though it was difficult to tell for sure) were indeed gone. By now, Jess was beginning to suspect that Lady Luck might not in fact have cut them a break here after all.

Of the drums that remained, only three were, by their positions, contenders for the one in which Sally had taken refuge, and with her heart thumping, Jess hauled the lid off the first of them.

It was full of ore.

She opened the second.

More ore.

Finally, number three.

And as Jess took in the ore-packed interior of the third drum, she felt her guts twist with fear. Cos yup, no question about it now. Lady L, true to her long-established form, had flipped them the finger, sashayed her bitch-like way out of the building, and torched the place on the way out.

8

Lovelight

From somewhere outside the freight wagon came the male voice Jess had heard before. "Okay, let's go," it said, and turning at the sound, Jess crept her way up to the wagon's open side door, easing her head around its grimy metal edge. Outside was a world of rutted concrete and rusting steel—the grim, harshly lit interior of some kind of covered loading dock—and as her eyes followed the sound of the departing voices, Jess spotted at the far end of the dock two overall-clad men steering a steam-powered hydraulic warehouse trolley. On the trolley were four ore drums, one of which, Jess needlessly reminded herself, currently contained the curled up and doubtless seething form of a lone deathwish-harboring idiot stowaway.

As Jess watched, the two men disappeared with their trolley through an archway set in the dock's far wall, and the instant they were gone, Jess stuck her head out a little farther through the open door of the freight car, scanning the rest of the area for any other signs of scumbag humanity. Upon finding none, she gulped back her rising fear and then hopped down from the wagon to the concrete floor outside, glancing all about her.

The loading dock in its entirety turned out to be considerably larger than Jess had been expecting, the robbers' diesel loco parked in one of several lengthy bays, all eleven trucks of its stolen cargo still hitched behind. For a gang of lowlife outlaws, these people looked incredibly well organized, Jess thought. Unfortunately, such organization would likely extend to their security measures too, for which read 'big guys with bigger guns'. And that was *not* good, seeing as how Jess's own personal armory currently consisted of a single pajama cord and a couple of scrunchies with barely any stretch left in them. All things considered, she *really* didn't fancy her chances in a showdown, even if Sally could probably have eliminated an entire troop of bad guys using the same equipment.

Jess turned once more to peer in the direction

the two men had gone. *Okay,* she thought, *Element of Surprise it is then,* and gulping back her fear for a second time, she set off, slinking her way through the loading dock towards the archway the men had vanished into.

• • •

"Well, golly, aren't *we* clever," Vera said, glancing down at the garish pink and silver advertising flyer in Declan's hands—the one he'd plucked from the cork noticeboard not a quarter of an hour ago—then up at the garish pink and silver shop front the three of them stood before.

"Go us," Dave agreed.

The shop in question—just two minutes' walk from a convenient siding wherein now rested an idling Cannonball Express—stood situated near the center of a typical small town main drag, the building's eye-popping décor adding an outrageous touch of glamor to what was otherwise the very epitome of frontiersville nondescript. The effect was, Vera thought, not unlike encountering a cupcake on a shelf full of stale bread rolls. With the glittery logo on the shop's sign—*'Lovelight's Veterinary Services'*—replicated in miniature on the advertising leaflet Declan held out before them, that they'd come to the right place was beyond question, though if further confirmation *had* been needed, the immaculate pink pickup truck on whose driver's side door they had first seen the *'Lovelight's'* logo stood parked by the front of the shop, looking, if anything, even *more* immaculate and pink than it had before.

"Okay, let me handle this," Declan said and, adopting a kind of macho 'bad cop' attitude, was just stepping forward to approach the shop when, all at once, through its open door, there came a monstrous, blood-freezing screech. Protracted, high-pitched, and aching with animal emotion, it was a cry unlike anything Vera had ever heard— the kind of plaintive, ear-piercing squeal she imagined a giant mutant bat might have made upon seeing the love of its life marry another.

And then, as if monstrous unidentified screeches weren't enough, what followed was something that, in the circumstances, seemed almost *more* disturbing to Vera. Music. If she wasn't very much mistaken, the string-drenched intro section of *Next to You* by cartoon queen of the flapper age Betsy Bow.

It was at that point a slightly unsettled look entered Declan's eye. Entered *all* their eyes, if truth be told. But then, rallying manfully with a tough guy crick of the neck, Declan resumed his purposeful march and stomped on through the front door of the vet's shop, a still visibly nervous Dave trotting along behind.

Drawing in a deep breath, Vera followed,

stepping through the door into a tiny but well-appointed vet's surgery, primly decorated (in pink and silver) with satin throw cushions, cutesy cat pictures, and enough lace doilies to satisfy an entire Martian colony of maiden aunts. Vera did find herself questioning whether such a thing as a spittoon could ever really warrant the delicate services of a doily, but quibbles aside, the overall effect was, she had to admit, a style statement of singular boldness. If anyone ever wished to know what it was like to live *inside* a cupcake, this, Vera reckoned, was as close as they were likely to get.

"With you in a moment, my lovelies," a disincarnate voice chimed, subsequently incarnating itself in the form of a bespectacled and neatly attired little man who popped up from behind the massive workbench that occupied the center of the room. Vera saw immediately that it was the same fellow they'd spotted at the refinery last night—the one who had driven the woman away in Barbie's own pickup truck.

Declan opened his mouth to speak, but before he could, the little man raised a finger, politely indicating that, for the nonce, silence would be appreciated. Somewhat nonplussed (and with 'bad cop' apparently clocking off for the time being), Declan duly shut his mouth and stood there mute while the man before them proceeded to remove a pair of heavy canvas covers from two large square objects that rested on the workbench.

The objects turned out to be cages, each one containing a single giant beetle-like lifeform possessed of glittering compound eyes, massive serrated mandibles, and significantly more legs than Vera thought acceptable in any living organism. As the canvas covering was whipped from the cage that held the larger of the two creatures (*considerably* larger, Vera noted, at almost a full meter long), said creature let out a loud, plaintive squeal—the same one they'd heard from outside—and began immediately to throw itself against the bars of its metal prison.

"There there, my lovely, not long now," the vet cooed to the bug monster, before going on to pull the drapes of the surgery's single window and light four candles, one at each corner of the workbench. With the syrupy violins still emanating from a gramophone in the corner, and soft candlelight now the only illumination, the result was a kind of sickly romantic atmosphere that seemed to please the vet. After a satisfied nod, he went on to shift one of the cages until it abutted the other, following which he fastened both together using a pair of sturdy steel clips. Meanwhile, from the gramophone in the corner, Betsy Bow began to croon in her nasal New York twang:

"Some might say I got the frog and not the prince;

That a face like yours
Deserves the coldest shoulder.
But the Laws of Love apply,
And they'd see a different guy
If they viewed you through the eye
Of this beholder..."

Studying the smaller, less agitated of the two creatures, the little vet tutted in a kind of prissy disapproval, before reaching for a shelf behind him and removing from it something that looked like a gardener's spraygun. Printed on the gun's side were the letters 'UPS', and tutting still, the vet raised the spraygun towards the smaller bug monster, giving the creature a hefty squirt of the gun's colorless liquid contents. The result of this action was as instantaneous as it was pronounced: all at once, the larger creature appeared finally to notice the smaller one in the cage next door and began to throw itself in that direction, its monstrous mewling growing louder as it surged against the bars separating it from its excessively legged fellow. At the same time, the smaller creature began to stir, registering the larger's ever-more-urgent attentions even as Betsy's squeaky serenade arrived at the song's popular refrain:

"Next to you Valentino is an ordinary Joe.

Next to you Rudy Vallee ain't so hot.
Handsome boys? Oh, for sure.
They got bags of allure.
But despite all their voodoo
They can't turn my head like you do..."

With the larger of the beetle organisms now pressing itself hard against the intervening bars, the vet proceeded to pull away the removable cage panels that kept the two creatures apart, and no longer separated, the bigger monster at last scuttled through to pounce on the smaller. Little more than half the size of the creature that fell upon it, the small beetle monster submitted immediately, and the gruesome pair went on to writhe together in a conspicuously sensual embrace, the screech of their insect cries and the stick-like clatter of their way-too-many legs providing an unlikely counterpoint to Betsy's adenoidal crooning:

"Next to you they ain't nothin',
And while most won't think it so,
They don't see you the way that I do.
You've a queer sort of glamor,
And my heart beats like a hammer...
So perplexed
When I'm next
To you..."

As the music continued, and the two creatures proceeded to mate—because there could be no doubt now about what was going on here—the vet offered Vera and the others a mischievous smile, before glancing again fondly at the writhing bug monsters. "Soft lights and a little bit of Betsy," he whispered to Vera with a wink. "Well *I* would, wouldn't *you?*"

While Vera stood wondering if there existed any reality in which, under similar circumstances, such a remark could ever receive a coherent reply, the little man, apparently sensing the group's bewilderment, doffed an imaginary cap and, with the most courteous and elfin of bows, finally introduced himself:

"Isaac Lovelight, at your service. How may I help, my lovelies?"

9

Bad Cop, VERY Bad Cop

Just as Vera began to wonder exactly how long the perplexed silence in the vet's surgery might spin on, Declan had a shot at a response. With another tough guy crick of the neck, 'Bad Cop' clocked back in and took a step forward. But even as the Irishman opened his mouth to speak, Isaac Lovelight gave a theatrical wince, indicated once again the mating bug creatures on the workbench, then raised a finger to signal that Declan may proceed only if he did so *quietly*.

Apparently unprepared to indulge in anything so unmanly as whispering, 'Bad Cop' exited the scene for a second time, leaving an awkward

Declan to clear his throat, shuffle a bit, and murmur to the pixie-like fellow in the gold-rimmed spectacles, "Okay, well, um, maybe you remember us from yesterday? At the refinery?"

"The refinery, my love?" the little vet whispered back, cocking his head to one side.

"Yes. We were there loading up some uranium ore. You were there with a woman."

"I'm sorry, lovely, I don't follow."

"A woman who seemed particularly keen on acquiring our cargo."

At this, Vera saw a distinctly wary look creep into the vet's twinkling blue eyes. "Ah... yes," the little man whispered to Declan. "Yes, I remember now."

"Well, good. Because we need to know who that woman was."

Lovelight's perfectly manicured fingernails began to drum on the workbench beside him. "Well, um," he said, "of course, I'm not sure I'm exactly at liberty to *say* who——"

Declan drew in a sharp breath, clearly teeing up some angry interruption, but again Lovelight raised a finger, nodding to the bizarre insect seduction still playing out next to them.

This time though, Declan batted the vet's finger away. "*Enough!*" he barked, ignoring the creatures and taking a step forward to press his substantial chest into Isaac Lovelight's face. In

Declan's defense, neither lovebug appeared to take the slightest notice of any of this, the larger of the monsters now apparently well past second base, as far as Vera was able to make out through the jiggling, clicking forest of insect legs.

Trapped between shirtfront and workbench, Isaac Lovelight strove to shore up his professional smile while Declan continued unhushed:

"Last night, our entire cargo of uranium ore was stolen. Every single wagon. And if you think this woman might have had something to do with that, I'd advise you to tell us so, right now."

At last, Vera saw Lovelight's smile falter. "Oh... no no no," the man said, "I'm sure she would never have... no no no..." and lowering his gaze, the little vet squirmed free then bustled off to the other side of the workbench, refocusing his attention on the two cavorting bug monsters as the Betsy Bow record played out its final bars:

> *"You've a queer sort of glamor,*
> *And my heart beats like a hammer...*
> *So perplexed,*
> *Sweetly vexed,*
> *And profoundly oversexed*
> *When I'm next*
> *To you."*

—upon   which   concluding   phrase,   and

choreographed almost to perfection with the romantic violin coda that ended the record, the larger monster gave a final sensuous quiver and bit the head off its mate, green goo spraying and assorted entrails erupting as the smaller creature went instantly limp.

With a motherly beneficence worthy of the Virgin Mary herself, Isaac Lovelight beamed down at the surviving bug monster and purred, "There we are, my lovely lady. Now wasn't he worth waiting for?" following which the large beetle creature began at once to eat the remains of the smaller specimen in a gorge-inducing symphony of slurps, snaps, and dull crunching.

"GM dung beetle breeding program," the little vet finally offered by way of explanation, once more turning his elfin smile on Vera and the boys. "For the local recycling company. Aren't they just *the* most adora—"

"Okay, that is *it!*" Vera snapped, surprising herself with the red hot rage that came surging up into her chest. "Now you just listen to me, young fellow m'lad," and throwing open the curtains to flood the room with light, Vera stormed up to the surgery's startled owner, jabbing a furious forefinger into the topmost button of his waistcoat. "Right now, two very close chums of mine might be at the mercy of whichever no-good ruffians had the gall to steal our cargo last night."

From the corner of her eye, Vera spotted an equally startled Declan and Dave share a gawp before mouthing the word *Ruffians???* to each other. And yes, three question marks were most certainly implied in the boys' silent exchange.

Undeterred, Vera plowed on. "These are people I care about deeply, matey," she said to Lovelight, accompanying the remark with a further emphatic jab from Peter Pointer. "The chums, that is, not the ruffians. Which, I imagine, is obvious in context. And by 'care about deeply' I mean platonically, of course, rather than... where was I?" Okay, this was *not* going quite as Vera had hoped, and as if to confirm the same, she saw a series of none-the-wiser frowns bounce back and forth between the three men in the room.

Eventually, Isaac Lovelight cleared his throat and resumed his feeble excuses: "Look, I really am sorry, my lovely, but I took an oath. Vet/client privilege demands that——"

And once again, that unexpected fury rose like boiling lava in Vera's chest, prompting her this time to reach for and grab the plastic spraygun device Lovelight had used on the smaller bug monster. Wielding the thing as if it were a Magnum, Vera proceeded to pump the device's trigger repeatedly and with force, dowsing Lovelight in copious quantities of the spraygun's contents.

Coughing and spluttering and flapping at the air around him, the little vet staggered backwards several steps until he was out of range, then began to wipe himself down. "What— what— what do you think you're doing?" he stammered, his wide eyes fixed on Vera.

As it happened, the vet wasn't the only one mystified by Vera's actions:

"Um, yeah, actually," Dave interjected, "I was just about to ask the same thing."

Declan raised a hesitant *me too* finger.

Jutting out her chin in defiance, Vera shoved the spraygun in Dave and Declan's direction so they could both read the writing on it. "UPS," she declared with a dark satisfaction she should probably have felt guilty about but absolutely did not. "Universal Pheromone Substitute. Vets and breeders all over Mars use it to assist in… reproductive matters. It's programmed chemically with a DNA sample from the species you want to… assist." At this, Vera allowed her gaze to dart to the surviving beetle monster in the two conjoined cages—the one now gobbling down the last of its unfortunate mate—and it was then that the creature itself seemed finally to take note of developments, whirling where it crouched and once again throwing itself at the bars of its prison, this time in the direction of Dr. I. Lovelight BVM. A second round of monstrous

66

squealing began to rend the air of the surgery, the creature's massive, goo-slathered mandibles clattering against metal as they reached through the bars for the horrified vet.

"I'll be honest," Vera resumed, turning to address Lovelight again, "I can't claim to be overly knowledgeable in such matters, but unless I am drastically misreading the signals here, *that*—" and she nodded to the writhing bug creature in the cage "—is *not* a picture of a lady whose itch has been comprehensively scratched. As it were. So to speak. By which I mean to imply—"

"Yeah, pretty sure the fella gets it," Declan said.

"Well, jolly good," Vera acknowledged with a curt dip of her head, "because unless the 'fella' in question furnishes us with the information we require, and does so promptly, comprehensively, and with good grace..." Vera unfastened one of the two steel clips holding the joined cages together, made as if to unfasten the second... and watched Isaac Lovelight shrink back with a horrified whimper.

"Fleet-footed little blighters, these things look to me," Vera continued, forced to raise her voice now, so that she might be heard above the sound of the ladybug's frenzied shrieking. "*You,* on the other hand," and she cast a further glance over the trembling vet before her, "do not look at all like a fellow with a track record in running. For your life or otherwise."

Lovelight gulped, no doubt regretting with a passion that same lack of track record.

"So…" Vera said with a let's-wind-this-up smile, her hands reaching once more for the second clip, "… would you two like some romantic music perhaps or…?"

●●●

Fewer than five minutes later, Vera sat in a rear corner of the Cannonball's cab alongside one extremely nervous veterinary surgeon, while at the front of the cab, Declan shoveled coal and Dave manned the controls of the speeding loco, now thundering on to a fresh destination.

Since leaving Isaac Lovelight's surgery and reboarding the Cannonball with their new, albeit reluctant accomplice, Vera couldn't help but note that both Dave and Declan had been unusually quiet, and upon looking across at the pair now, she was amused to catch Declan glancing over his shoulder at her with an expression that looked ever so slightly… *fearful.*

In response, Vera raised a single questioning eyebrow at the fellow, and Declan hurriedly resumed his shoveling, the Cannonball steaming onward through the Martian morning.

10

Highly Corrosive

Hugging the shadows by one wall, Jess made her way along the dark corridor, in silent pursuit of the two men and their trolley full of uranium ore drums. The rickety trundle of the trolley's wheels echoed down the passageway, and a harsh chemical smell clung to the dank air, its acrid tang biting deeper into Jess's lungs the farther down the corridor she crept.

Around twenty or so meters from a closed double door at the passageway's end, the two men wheeling the trolley stopped suddenly, and Jess felt her stomach clench, sure that Sally had somehow given away her presence in one of the four drums. Ducking out of sight down a shallow alcove in the corridor wall, Jess held her breath as she watched the man at the head of the trolley frown, reach for one of the ore drums…

… and then begin simply to adjust the drum's placement, repositioning it a little, as if it might have been wobbly and threatening to topple.

Jess breathed out and sank back against the broad metal door that filled the alcove she'd ducked into for cover. But her relief was short-lived, because at that very same moment, there came from behind Jess a kind of low, rumbling roar—a sound so deep it almost wasn't a sound at all but a physical, gut-churning tremble, the thunderous depth of it shaking the surface of the door Jess's back was pressed against. Whirling where she stood, Jess cast a startled eye over the heavy steel rectangle of the door itself, and as the corridor around her continued to shake with that unearthly bellow, she pressed her nose against the door's tiny, eye-level window, peering into the shadows beyond it.

What she saw in those shadows sent Jess's already pounding heart lurching northwards, and it was all she could do to stifle a cry of shock. Staggering back a step, she almost stumbled out into the passageway again, straight into full view of the men with the trolley. Only one hastily flung hand saved the day as, with it, she managed to grab the door's thick steel handle and haul herself back into her hiding place.

Jess gulped. That was too close. *Way* too close. *Dammit,* but she *had* to keep it together here…

Moments later, as the monstrous roar began at last to diminish, Jess heard the men again:

"Okay, all good," one of them said, "let's go," and peeking round the edge of her alcove, Jess saw the two guys head off once more, wheeling the trolley for the door at the end of the corridor.

Heart still kicking against her ribcage, Jess resumed her pursuit, swallowing down the last of her shock and slinking back into the shadows that flanked the dimly lit passageway. Even as she went though, Jess's eyes, almost against her will, darted back one final time to the window in the alcove door, where they caught themselves a last parting glimpse of the jaw-dropping horror that lurked behind it. Just a detail this time—a monstrous wall of pulsing, glistening skin that rose into view, pressed itself against the glass of the window, and then, even as that hellish rumbling cry finally died to silence, receded once more into the dark.

Yet again, Jess was forced to gulp back her rising terror. Because seriously, what the hell kind of train robbers needed something like *that* to hijack the fifteen-thirty to New Detroit?

Up ahead, Jess watched the men wheel their laden trolley towards and then through the double doors that terminated the corridor, the pair eventually disappearing from view as, with a reverberating clatter, the two doors swung shut again behind them.

Fortunately, both of *those* doors also sported small windows, so after edging her way up to them, Jess peeked through into the space beyond, weighing up her chances of entering unseen.

And those chances, it seemed, were good. The area on the other side of the double doors—some kind of laboratory, it looked like—was, for now, sparsely populated, said population consisting of the two trolley guys (currently facing away from the entrance as they walked on) and only two further occupants. Luckily for Jess, both of *those* occupants *also* stood with their backs to the door, the likelihood that either would spot someone sneaking in reduced still further by what the two individuals wore—full-body hazmat suits topped with vision-restricting masks.

Edging open one of the double doors, Jess slunk silently through the gap and ducked down behind some fortuitously placed packing crates to assess the area and her options.

About twenty or so meters square, the laboratory (if such it turned out to be) was rigged floor to ceiling and wall to wall with an intricate network of steel pipes, along with towering gantries, hissing hydraulics, and a complex array of moving conveyer belts. The acrid chemical smell was even *more* pronounced in here than in the corridor outside, Jess noted, and she could certainly understand the need of hazmat suits for anyone working in the place longer than a few minutes at a time.

Crouched behind the crates, Jess watched the two trolley men park their machine by a floor level section of conveyor belt, grab one of the ore drums between them, and hoist it onto the broad moving ribbon of black plastic. Seconds later, the drum was gone, pulled by the belt through a dark opening in a metal wall that was hung with workaday factory tools—brooms, mops, ladders, fire blankets. The rest of the drums followed quickly, after which the two men wheeled their now empty trolley away again, disappearing with it through the double doors they'd entered by.

Eyeing the dark opening the ore drums had vanished through, and after checking that she remained unobserved by the pair in hazmat suits, Jess made a dash for it, darting from her hiding place behind the crates and up to the section of conveyer where the trolley men had offloaded the four drums. But just as she was about to leap aboard the belt itself and follow the drums through into the dark, something high up snagged Jess's attention, and raising her eyes, she saw the first of the ore drums reappear on another section of conveyer, this one almost ten meters above.

While Jess crouched there watching, the moving belt carried the drum to the conveyor's end and jerked to a stop, following which a hissing, hydraulic robo-arm came swinging in from still higher above. Rattling and clanking, the claw attachment on the arm's end quickly popped the lid of the waiting drum, discarded the same lid through a nearby slot, and then went on to lift the entire drum from the belt. With a further series of creaks and clanks, the robo-arm swung the drum out past the end of the paused conveyer…

… and that was when Jess finally took in what lay beneath the now open-topped barrel in the robo-arm's grip.

It was a huge vat, also open-topped and filled with some kind of clear liquid. Beside the vat, the two hazmat-suited workers looked on, and for the first time, Jess heard one of them speak:

"You might wanna step back a bit, Joe," the guy said, voice muffled by the full-face mask of his suit.

"Yeah, sorry," his colleague replied. "Hang on a sec. Just dropped my—" and raising a pair of long plastic tongs, the man reached out with them to retrieve something from the massive vat of liquid. At first, Jess failed to recognize what the retrieved object was, but then it clicked. It was nothing more remarkable than your basic office-style clipboard, except that this particular example, made of some kind of gray metal, was smoldering visibly, half of it apparently eaten away by whatever the vat contained.

Even as Jess was choking back a cry of horror, the two hazmat guys stepped back together from the huge vat of liquid, revealing at last the stark red warning sign on its side:

DANGER!
CONCENTRATED HYDROCHLORIC ACID
HIGHLY CORROSIVE!

If Jess thought her ribcage had taken a kicking from her shocked heart before, it was nothing compared to the assault it suffered now. "Oh god, no," she gasped, her eyes shooting upwards to the ore drum in the robo-claw above. The ore drum now lidless and dangling directly over a giant vat of nature's most corrosive solvent.

And then, before Jess could even snatch a breath, let alone call out, the hydraulic arm tipped up the barrel in its claw—

—and a load of heavy, half-caked uranium ore powder went splashing into the vat, sizzling and smoking as it sank beneath the acid. Seconds later, the robo-arm began to shake the drum, as if to dislodge the last of the ore inside, and as further quantities of the yellow powder cascaded into the vat below, Jess saw the high conveyer belt restart, the rest of the ore drums reappearing now in a neat line, all three headed, there could be no doubt, for exactly the same fate as the first.

Jess had no choice. Leaping into full view of the men in hazmat suits, she yelled, "SALLY! GET OUTTA THERE! GET OUTTA THERE NOW!"

With yells of their own, the two lab workers spun in Jess's direction. "What the hell—"

"Stop it!" Jess roared at the men. "Stop the machine! There's somebody in one of the—"

She never finished the sentence. Because just then, even as the robo-claw removed the lid from Drum Number Two, the lid of the *third* drum behind it popped off by itself, and there was Sally—bedhead hair, tattered babydoll, eyes squinting in the harsh white light of the laboratory.

"Jess? Is that you?" Sally hollered, prompting still more cries of shock from the two lab guys.

"Oh my god! Stop the process!" the first shouted, his yell sending Hazmat Two racing for a control panel at the opposite end of the lab.

Sally's head whirled left and right. "Jess?" she shouted again. "Where are you? What the hell's going—" and that was when she seemed finally to take in her situation—the moving conveyer belt, the clanking robo-arm, the vat of fizzing, smoking liquid below.

"Oh boy," Sally said, "this is *not* good..."

11

The Perils of Sally

Frozen with terror, and while Hazmat Two sprinted for the lab's distant control panel, Jess watched helpless as Sally braced her arms against the sides of the ore drum, preparing to leap free. But the mechanical claw came swinging in again, forcing Sally to duck back into the drum and then blocking her escape as it executed its now redundant attempt to remove the drum lid that was no longer there. Seconds later, the claw seized the barrel in its metal fingers and hoisted it from the paused conveyor with Sally still inside.

"NO!" Jess bellowed, unable to do anything but watch in horror as the robo-claw swung out over the vat of acid, jerked to a stop, and then tipped the barrel up.

A blur of black satin and flailing limbs came tumbling from the open end of the inverted drum, and Jess screamed in shock. But somehow, Sally managed to twist in mid-air, her fingers grabbing the rim of the upside-down drum's open end, her plunging body slumping to a stop. Bare legs pedaling at the empty air, Sally clung on by her literal fingertips, the rippling surface of the acid not eight meters beneath her jerking feet.

"Oh god! Halt the process!" Hazmat Number One shrieked. "Halt it NOW!"

"I have done!" his colleague yelled back, wrenching lever after lever on the control panel he stood before. "It has to complete the sequence first! There's nothing else I can——"

Then the robo-claw began to shake the ore drum, and Sally let out a roar, the muscles of her forearms bulging, her face twisting with exertion as she fought to maintain a hold on the rim of the shaking barrel. But even from where Jess stood below, she could already see that hold starting to loosen, and just five seconds later, it gave way altogether, Sally's screaming form plummeting like a rock for the vat of acid beneath.

If, during that same five seconds, Jess had not managed to snatch a long ladder from the lab wall and thrust it over the top of the vat to break Sally's fall, the gal would surely have been signing out for good. Even as it was, the horror was far from over, Sally's arms and legs slipping *through* the rungs of the ladder-slash-bridge, her fingers and toes coming to a stop just centimeters above the surface of the acid.

"Sally! To me!" Jess yelled. "*Now, Sal!*"

Groaning in pain, Sally pulled her arms and legs back up through the rungs of the ladder and rose onto her hands and knees—

—only to be slammed flat again as the robo-arm above her upended the fourth and final drum, its contents crashing hard into Sally's back. The impact of the near solid mass of caked ore powder, along with the rebound that followed, almost bounced Sally straight off the ladder into the acid, and with another cry of shock, Jess lunged forward, shoving the whole of her upper body down onto the end of the ladder that protruded past the vat's circular rim. Praying it would be enough to brace the makeshift bridge, Jess beckoned wildly to her friend:

"Sally! To me! I gotcha!"

With eyes dazed and bloodshot, Sally looked up, rose again onto all fours, and began at last to scramble her way forward over the rungs of the ladder, heading for Jess. A heartbeat later, Jess reached out, grabbed Sally's wrists, and with one desperate yank, the pair of them went tumbling backwards, slumping into a heap on the floor of the lab.

"Oh god, Sal," Jess gasped as they both struggled to their feet. "Are you okay?"

It was at that point that Sally—her chest heaving, her pajama-clad frame caked in yellow ore powder—finally clocked the bright red warning sign on the side of the vat, and at the sight of it the gal just sighed, shaking her head in a kind of weary disbelief. "Acid?" she said. "You have *got* to be kidding me," and turning where she stood, she shot a dangerous glower at Hazmat Number One, the fella now stumbling up to them and pulling off his mask to reveal a youthful face as confused as it was terrified. "What the hell *is* this, dude?" Sally spat at the wide-eyed Hazmat One. "The Perils of frickin Pauline!" following which she slammed a powder-caked fist into the guy's chin, and Hazmat One went down like the proverbial sack of King Edwards, consciousness taking an impromptu vacation.

"Um, to be fair, Sal," Jess said, "they both did just try to, you know... *help?*"

Sally gave vent to a further exhausted sigh and turned thoughtfully to Hazmat Number Two, said fella also approaching now, though with noticeably more caution than his colleague and with both hands raised in apparent surrender.

"Help? *Really?*" Sally said, considering the

second guy carefully for another moment...

... before taking him out as well with a brutal roundhouse to the head. Hazmat Two flew backwards several meters and slumped atop his colleague, where, like that previous unfortunate, he remained strongly disinclined to take any further part in the proceedings.

"So I'm a grouch," Sally said to Jess. "Sue me. Now let's go get our damn cargo back," and turning as one, Jess and Sal took off, the ore-caked Ms. Chu shedding clumps of yellow powder as the pair of them flew on through the double doors, back out into the corridor.

12

Escape

As the Cannonball thundered on through the rocky red terrain of northern Mars, Vera, to her surprise, found herself feeling a trifle sorry for the diminutive veterinarian seated beside her in the cab. More bewildered than anything else, the fellow's reluctance to talk had long since departed, and bellowing over the clatter of the wheels and the bustle of Dave and Declan as they worked the loco's controls, Isaac Lovelight continued in his earnest efforts to explain:

"... so even if Sara *did* borrow your cargo—and I'm not saying she *did*—but *if* she did, you have to understand the position she was in. Still *is* in..."

●●●

Bare feet pounding rutted concrete, Jess and Sally sprinted through the dark, back down the corridor that had led to the laboratory. By Jess's reckoning, they'd reach the loading dock in under a minute, and once there (and provided they didn't run into any resistance), firing up the robbers' diesel then escaping in it with the cargo would be the work of just a minute more.

Powering along at Jess's shoulder, Sally frowned as she ran. "Okay, babe, you know *none* of this makes any sense, right? What kind of scumbag train robbers need a facility like *this?* What the hell even *is* this place anyway? Some kinda mining operation, maybe?"

"No maybe about it," Jess shot back, pulling up by the alcove she'd hid in when following the trolley guys, then nodding to its heavy steel door as Sally came to a stop beside her. "Take a look, but be quick."

Sally pressed her nose against the door's window… and her eyes widened. "Okaaaaay. Beginning to see the light a little now. So if these people are actually—"

But before she could finish, the same nightmarish roar from earlier rang out once again, shaking the corridor like a not-so-minor earthquake, and a moment later, just as it had before, a wall of monstrous skin surged into view behind the window, slamming against the solid steel of the door with enough impact to send flakes of rust cascading from its corroded surface.

Recoiling in shock, Jess shot a glance at the floor, where clumps of the uranium ore that Sally continued to shed were starting to accumulate. The fine-ground powder stained the concrete like yellow paint, swirling in puddles of filthy water that pooled in corners of the alcove and seeped beneath the steel door, carrying the yellow powder along with it.

Another earth-shaking cry sent still more tremors rattling along the empty corridor, and this time the thud that followed at the alcove door was bigger. *Much* bigger. Jess saw the heavy steel panel—surely eight centimeters thick—actually *bend* under the assault.

"Whoah!" was the most Sally could manage before the pair of them took off again down the passageway, the sounds of the creature—its roars as well as its colossal thrashing—crescendoing all around as Jess and Sal fled for the loading dock.

● ● ●

In the cab of the speeding Cannonball, Vera and the boys listened with reluctant but growing fascination as Isaac Lovelight continued: "The main problem is they haven't hit a seam for over a year

84

now. Business-wise, it's been calamitous for Sara. She's already had to lay off nearly half her workforce. But even *that's* not the worst of it. Not even *close* to the worst..."

• • •

Jess let Sally take the lead as the pair of them raced into the loading dock. Bracing herself for what they might have to face there, Jess was once again surprised at the dearth of personnel. Only two overall-clad engineers had appeared since Jess had sneaked her way out of the dock in pursuit of the trolley men. Even better, both of those engineers were facing *away* from the door, engrossed in their work on the diesel as Jess and Sally came flying into the cavernous compound.

Way too late, one of the engineers gave a startled yell and spun, her eyes widening in shock as she took in the pajama-clad forms of Jess and Sal barreling at her. "Huh? Who the hell are—"

Jess could all but see the comic book BAM! and POW! as Sally took out the defenseless duo with a single swift combo. *Damn,* but it was about time Jess learned to do stuff like that.

Bolting for the front of the diesel, Jess pulled open the driver's door and was just about to leap onto the cab's access steps when the single most heart-stopping roar yet rumbled through the loading dock. At the same time, something seemed to slam into a long section of breezeblock wall at the far end of the compound. Something on the wall's other side. Something *big.*

No prizes for guessing what, Jess thought, and trading further panicked looks with Sal, she hauled herself up into the diesel's cab and lunged for the controls.

•••

"The plain fact is, the industry relies on them almost entirely now. As far as intelligence goes, they may only have the brain of an earthworm, but with uranium ore their sole natural food source, the ability of these animals to seek out rich seams in surrounding rock is priceless. Unfortunately, in the case of this *particular* creature..." Isaac Lovelight sighed. "The poor thing hasn't eaten for over a year. It's quite literally *starving...*"

•••

In the cab of the robbers' diesel, while Sal kept lookout through the windows, Jess released the brake lever, punched the loco's starter, and felt the engine rumble to life around her. With a dark smile, she opened the throttle and was rewarded with a satisfying lurch as locomotive and cargo started forward at once. Seconds later, the train was accelerating hard, clattering over points as it sped towards the loading dock's exit.

"And yet... *still* no team of shouty dudes with buzz cuts and big guns," Sally yelled to Jess over the engine noise, her head stuck out a side window, "which, call me old-fashioned, I admit to finding *slightly* dissatisfying. That said, we *do* seem to be losing some cargo, babe..."

Jess shoved her own head out the window nearest her, glancing towards the rear of the train in time to see an ore drum go tumbling from the open side door of the very last freight wagon—the wagon whose cargo had been unstrapped by the trolley guys, Jess remembered. At the same time, clouds of yellow ore powder—presumably from the drums Jess herself had pulled the lids off when looking for Sal—began to vent from the same gaping doorway, sucked through in billowing plumes as the train raced for the exit.

And all the while, behind the breezeblock wall at the far end of the dock, that no-prizes-for-guessing-what continued to slam itself against ever-more-crumbling brickwork...

●●●

"Under normal circumstances, emergency intravenous feeding would usually be employed over lean periods like this—basically, a solution of highly refined uranium ore in concentrated hydrochloric acid. But with the current uranium shortage in the region, I think Sara just found herself in an impossible position…"

•••

Jess hauled back harder still on the throttle, and as the loco surged up to the loading dock's exit, yet another stupendous roar shook the air. This time though, it was accompanied by an apocalyptic crash, and from the window she peered through, Jess saw the entire wall on the far side of the dock finally give way in an avalanche of breezeblock and steelwork and roiling cement dust. For just a split-second more, Jess saw something else there too— the creature responsible for that shocking destruction, vast and black, heaving amongst the dust and debris—then the view was lost as the train cleared the exit and raced out of the loading dock into bright Martian daylight.

•••

Isaac Lovelight shook his head, his voice barely audible now over the rumble of the speeding Cannonball. "She was *desperate,* my loves, don't you see? If the trillopax dies, Sara's company dies too, along with the entire town the company supports. So if she did do what you *think* she did, surely you can understand her reasons, yes?"

Vera *did* understand. From the looks of it, Declan did too. Not Dave though:

"Okay, look," the boy from Staines blurted,

"just ol' Dave being the Arthur Dent of the group as usual, but what the *hell* is a *trillopax?*"

Vera turned to Dave to explain... but in the end, she never got the chance. Because just then, from up ahead, there came a sound—a *roar*—of such mind-boggling immensity it seemed all but to obliterate reality, setting the very air atremble and drowning out the thunder of the Cannonball's engine as if it were the buzzing of a gnat.

Vera's heart leapt in her chest, and reeling both physically and mentally, she hurled herself with the others at the loco's forward windows.

What she saw in those windows sent her reeling again.

Up ahead was a town. A *mining* town, Vera deduced from the industrial structures at its center. And hurtling from the exit of one of those structures was a locomotive—the very locomotive that had sped off with their cargo last night, still in fact hitched to those same stolen wagons. The train raced towards the Cannonball on a parallel track, some kind of yellow smoke billowing from its rearmost wagon, and not even fifty meters behind it, thundering along in apparent pursuit, was a vision of horror that seemed almost to defy reality.

Hurling itself forward on spiky black legs that must surely have numbered in their thousands, the trillopax looked to Vera like nothing so much as a titanic centipede, easily twice the length of the train it chased, twice the girth too. Its segmented black body gleamed like polished ebony, surging ahead in a series of hulking undulations, while its monstrous front end appeared to consist almost entirely of mouth—a vast toothed orifice that gaped ever wider as the colossal creature scrambled onto the track behind the fleeing train and began to close the distance between it and its diesel-powered quarry.

13

Trillopax

"Sally?" Jess bellowed over the tumultuous roar coming from behind the speeding diesel. "What's happening back there?"

"Girl, you do *not* wanna know," Sally yelled, her head still stuck out the side window, her mouth agape. "Just put your damn foot down!"

Chance would be a fine thing, Jess's failing brain offered as she stared helplessly at the control panel before her. Because the diesel's throttle was already at the end of its slot—had been ever since they'd cleared the exit of the loading dock. So what the hell were they supposed to do now?

Bracing herself for what she already knew she

would see, Jess took a deep breath and thrust her own head out a window to glance down the train. But for all the bracing, she gasped anyway, stunned rigid by her first unobstructed view of the horror on their tail. And the sheer *enormity* of the thing was only *half* that horror. The *other* half was how *fast* it was. The trillopax, despite its immense size, was already outpacing the diesel, its monstrous maw stretching wider with every meter the creature gained.

And then, even as Jess watched, the monster summoned yet *more* speed, surging forward with incredible acceleration until, mere moments later, its massive upper jaw came slamming down onto the train's ore-spewing rear wagon.

It felt like a bomb going off. The loco pitched, shuddered, almost left the rails altogether, and even at her near two hundred meters distance from the train's far end, Jess heard the crunch of compacting steel as the rearmost freight truck crumpled liked aluminum foil between the creature's gargantuan teeth. Seconds later, rear wagon still gripped tight in its mouth, the trillopax simply stopped where it was, dragging the entire train to a screeching, juddering halt.

The brutal deceleration sent both Jess and Sal cannoning forward in the diesel's cab, and flailing wildly, Jess rammed hard into the forward window. The slight give in the wide pane of toughened glass did absorb at least some of the impact for Jess, but Sally wasn't so lucky and hit the engine's solid steel control panel head first, slumping to the floor in a ragdoll heap.

•••

Peering through the binoculars she'd wrenched from a hook in the Cannonball's cab, it was all Vera could do not to scream as her mind struggled to accept what she was seeing. Now fewer than four hundred meters away, the diesel had come to a brutal halt, its rear wagon clamped fast in the trillopax's jaws. Which was shocking enough, but nothing compared to the horrifying *new* detail that Vera, through her binoculars, could alone make out. Because now, pressed flat against the diesel loco's broad front window, there was a figure. A single *pajama-clad* figure.

"Oh my god!" Vera blurted. "That's *Jess!*"

•••

Dazed and groaning, pain lancing through her battered skull, Jess peeled herself from the diesel's forward window, staggered back a step, and spun to Sally, still slumped and unmoving on the floor.

"Sally!" Jess yelled. "Sal!"

Not even a groan.

By now, all engine noise had ceased, and Jess could only imagine the damage their catastrophic stop had dealt to the loco's systems. However they were getting out of this nightmare, it would *not* be by diesel power.

"Sal!" Jess yelled again, and with still no reply, she grabbed her friend by the shoulders, shaking her hard. "Dammit, girl, get with the program!"

Nothing.

Cursing in fury, Jess began to drag the unconscious Sally towards the diesel's door, but had made it barely halfway there when the entire cab gave a sudden, violent lurch...

•••

... and this time Vera *did* scream, a shriek of both horror and disbelief as, with a single toss of its gargantuan head, the trillopax took the train's rear wagon into its mouth and gulped it down in one. The *complete wagon! In one!* Almost immediately, the rest of the diesel's eleven-truck cargo began to follow, the entire two hundred-meter-long shipment, drawn slowly, inexorably, gulp by gulp, truck by truck, into that gigantic toothed orifice.

From the corner of an eye, Vera caught a flash of movement beside her in the cab and turned to see Dave launch himself at the Cannonball's brake lever. A heartbeat later, deceleration sent all four of them slamming forward into the loco's main control array. Fountains of sparks cascaded past the side windows as locked drive-wheels shrieked over the rails beneath, and a full ten seconds later—to Vera it felt like ten *hours*—the Cannonball Express skidded to a jerking, smoking halt, just a wagon's length from where the diesel had come to its own stop on the parallel track.

Hauling herself from the forward window she'd ended up crushed against, Vera was the first out of the Cannonball, leaping from the loco's access ladder to the graveled trackside even as the three boys were still pulling themselves upright to follow. Smoke and steam from the Cannonball's emergency stop continued to billow around the locomotive in dense, acrid clouds, obscuring the view ahead, but Vera went bolting down the tracks regardless, racing for where she knew the diesel to be—where she knew her *friend* to be.

"Jess!" Vera roared. "Jess, get out of there! Get out of there now!"

Moments later, Vera hurtled clear of the smoke and steam—

—and the sight that met her eyes then almost stopped her heart.

More than three-quarters of the diesel's cargo had already disappeared down the tossing, convulsing gullet of the trillopax, still another of the trucks vanishing even as a helpless Vera stood watching. And with every gulp—with every wagon that vanished into that fleshy oblivion—the diesel loco itself was dragged farther and farther back down the track, jerk by brutal jerk, hauled ever closer to that monstrous, tooth-lined chasm. Worse yet, in the loco's forward window there was now no sign of Jess. None at all. And no sign of her trackside either.

"Oh god... JESS!" Vera yelled again. "GET OUT OF THERE!"

Behind her, Dave, Declan, and Lovelight finally came stumbling up, their own eyes starting in shock at the scene before them. Then they too began to shout, all four of them scrambling down the track, racing to close the distance between them and the retreating locomotive...

●●●

In the cab of the diesel, yet another violent lurch sent Jess crashing into a wall then slumping to the floor. With stars exploding across her vision like silent fireworks, she struggled to her feet once more and staggered back up to Sally, the gal still unmoving in a corner.

Hooking her hands beneath Sal's armpits, and with the cab pitching and shuddering around her, Jess began again to haul her unconscious friend towards the cab door—

—but just as Jess's fingers closed around the door handle, the loco gave its single most bone-shaking lurch yet, and with it came darkness, sudden and total, engulfing the entire cab...

●●●

Vera froze. Just stumbled to a stop with the others and stood there in shock as the last of the horror played out—as the diesel itself followed all eleven cargo trucks down the trillopax's clenching gullet.

"Oh god, NO!" Vera screamed, sagging to her knees in the dirt while her mind fought to reject the scene's ghastly parting image—an image so harrowing, so nightmarish, it would haunt Vera for the rest of her days. It was the image of Jess's desperate, bloodstained face, bobbing up for a split-second at the window of the diesel's door, just before the trillopax's massive jaws slammed shut over the front end of the loco, and the entire train was gone.

14

If Ever "Eeuuuw" Failed to Cover It

When it came to bad smells, Jess Flint imagined
herself to be a gal of broad experience.
Throughout her eighteen years on the red planet,
she had encountered a wide variety of unpleasant
odors, from mammoth dung to month-old dirty
laundry. But none of them—not even the unisex
toilets in the Lucky Horseshoe on a Saturday
night—had in any way prepared her for the no-
holds-barred violation of the nasal cavities she was
experiencing in the stygian darkness she now
found herself inhabiting. If the solar system's
rankest cheese factory had employed a workforce
of gangrenous zombies with toenail fungus and

gastro-intestinal issues, the place might have smelled a whole lot like this, Jess found herself thinking, all the while fighting to keep down the thankfully limited contents of her stomach.

All of which said, the *smell,* rank or otherwise, was, at this moment, far from Jess's most pressing problem. *That* would in fact be the aforementioned 'stygian darkness', and in an effort to deal with this first, Jess groped her way through the pitch black to the other side of the cab, her hands eventually locating the diesel's emergency locker on a wall panel by the engine controls. With a twist of its handle, the locker door clanked open, and moments later, Jess's probing fingers found what they were looking for.

Taking the long plastic tube in both hands, Jess bent it until she heard a dull snap, and after several vigorous shakes, a bright, green-tinged glow bloomed from the chemical lightstick, illuminating the cab interior.

Jess brought the glowing lightstick over to Sally, now stirring where she lay and groaning a little as she attempted to pull herself into a sitting position. Blood was starting to clot over a sizeable gash in Sally's forehead, the surrounding skin there bruised and blackening, but otherwise the gal would live, Jess reckoned. "Sal? Sal, you okay?"

Finally propping herself upright in a corner, Sally glanced about and then heaved a sigh of relief.

"Okay, great, we're still in the loco. At least we managed to get away from that thing."

"Um, well, about that," Jess said. "We——"

"Holy crap!" Sally blurted, scrunching up her nose in disgust. "What the *hell* is that *smell?*"

Heaving a sigh of her own, Jess was about to embark upon an explanation when Sally's blurting resumed, her gaze now directed over Jess's shoulder: "And what the *double* hell is *that?*"

Following Sally's two goggling eyes, Jess frowned, her heartrate stepping up a gear. Because 'that' turned out to be some kind of thick, gelatinous goo, seeping in the top half of the cab's partially open side window. Faintly translucent and greenish-brown in color, the goo fizzed and bubbled as it oozed down the interior wall of the cab, stripping away several layers of paint as it continued its icky journey south.

"At a guess," an unhappy Jess offered, "I'd say it was digestive acid."

For Sally, the penny dropped at last, and grabbing the lightstick from Jess, she struggled to her feet, raising the glowing baton to the cab's side window. Beyond the half open pane of toughened glass was a slick, bulbous wall of what appeared to be solid muscle, veined through with blood vessels and pulsing faintly in the green glow of the lightstick.

Sally shook her head in disbelief, her shoulders

slumping beneath the black satin of her babydoll. "Great," she said. "Just great. You realize we have already *done* acid today?"

Retrieving the lightstick from Sal, Jess bent the flexible tube into a hoop shape and hung it around her own neck. "To be fair," she said, "it *is* an entirely different kind of acid."

"Girl, you have got a *very* overdeveloped sense of what's fair. God-*dammit!*" Sally's curse was punctuated by a loud clang as her right fist slammed into a metal wall panel, the sound echoing through the cab. But then, only a second later, the gal drew in a slow deep breath, released it again even more slowly, and Jess watched the tension ebb from her friend's body as good ol' reliable take-charge-Sally re-entered the scene:

"Okay," Sal said. "It's cool. We got this, right? All we need to do is——"

Jess caught the blur of movement behind them just a second too late as something long and spiky and dripping with greenish-brown goo darted in the open side window, whipping around Sally's neck and choking the remainder of her words into a gurgle of shock.

"Oh my god!" Jess yelled, her hands, along with Sally's, flying to the worm-like monstrosity still slithering in the window and coiling itself around Sal's throat. Ignoring the sting of acid against her skin, and the icy stab of the creature's dense rows

101

of dorsal spines, Jess hauled with everything she had at the writhing tube of rubbery, slime-coated muscle. Sally did the same, and just as the monster's tail end came flopping in the window, their combined efforts won out. Wrenching the worm creature free of Sally's throat, they slammed the thing down onto the metal floor, where Sal's bare heel came stomping in at once, pulping the animal's head with an audible splat. Sally winced in pain and pulled her foot back from the creature, several of its spines now embedded in the fleshy pad of Sal's heel. For one more blood-freezing moment, Jess was sure that, headless or not, the still writhing worm monster was going to resume its attack. But then, after a couple more squirming, flopping death throes, the creature sagged into a pool of its own gunk and lay still.

Lifting her foot to inspect the damage to her heel, Sally yanked out several of the needle-like spines, blood oozing in dark droplets from the tiny puncture wounds left behind. "*Damn...*" was all the gal allowed herself as she tossed the bloodstained spikes aside in disgust.

For the next few moments, using corners of their ever-more-ragged nightwear, Jess and Sal did what they could to clean 'digestive acid' from areas of their skin that had been exposed to it, wiping the stuff away before it could blister them any more than it already had. It was only once this task was complete that the pair resumed inspection of their gruesome assailant, squinting in mutual revulsion at the corpse of the two-meter-long spiked worm atrocity.

"Seriously?" Sal said. "Ain't bad enough we get eaten by a monster? We have to deal with monsters *inside* the monster?"

Jess cocked her head at the nauseating remains by their feet, frowning in continued puzzlement. "Some kind of intestinal parasite, you think?"

"Jeez Louise," Sally murmured, "if ever 'eeuuuw' failed to cover it. I swear, girl, we——"

"Whoah!" Jess yelled, lunging forward a second time and slamming shut the cab's side window just as several more of the worm things slithered up to it, their fleshy undersides squelching against the glass, probing for an ingress that, thanks to Jess's quick reaction, was no longer there.

"And it's brought the wife and family," Sally sighed. "Nice."

"*Extended* family," Jess added as still more of the worm monsters began to appear. And not just at the side window either. *Other* windows in the cab seemed now to be attracting the things too, the animals squirming up in their dozens, their *hundreds* even. By the time Jess had finished scanning the full array of the loco's windows, every last one of them was covered, their toughened glass panels bulging inwards under the pressure of the countless creatures jammed against them. And it was a pressure that *continued* to grow, Jess couldn't help but observe, her racing mind conjuring up the disturbing image of yet more worm monsters piling in behind the ones already there, increasing that pressure even further...

"Okay," Sally said, "this is not looking—"

And that was when the side window finally gave way, a squirming deluge of slime and spikes and pale-fleshed horror pouring through into the cab.

Jess and Sally turned and fled.

Charging out through the cab's rear door, they bolted down the side corridor that ran the length of the diesel, then on into the crew car that was hitched directly behind. Jess hoped—*prayed*—they'd find at least *some* kind of refuge there...

... but no. At the crew car's windows, more of the parasites were already amassing, and before Jess and Sally had made it even halfway down the car's central aisle, glass shattered simultaneously in three of those windows, the nearest not four meters behind the fleeing pair. Another writhing cascade of spiked worm things came gushing in.

Barely two strides ahead of the nightmare tsunami, Jess and Sally charged onward for the door at the far end of the crew car. Slamming into it shoulder first, Jess hauled the door open, piled through, barged aside the door of the adjoining car, and went tumbling on into—

—some kind of maintenance wagon. Grimy tools and assorted chemical cans filled the myriad shelves and racks that lined the car's walls—walls that, unfortunately for Jess and Sal, also boasted several large windows, every one of them already straining under the pressure of the growing mass of worm creatures crushed against their glass. Jess and Sal had taken just four strides into the car when the first of those windows shattered. And not *behind* them like in the crew car, *up ahead*, forcing the pair to leap over the rush of vileness that spewed into the aisle to block their path.

As Jess's bare feet came slamming down on the far side of the writhing mass, she stumbled briefly, recovered, and then hurled herself on down the aisle, racing for the door at the maintenance car's far end. With Sally still hot on her heels, and just as two more of the car's windows exploded behind them, Jess reached the end door, wrenched it open, and plunged on through, leaping over the coupling mechanism that connected the rear of the maintenance wagon to what turned out to be the first of the stolen freight cars.

While more worm creatures surged up onto the coupler behind her, Jess yanked open the freight car's end door and was through in an instant, Sally right behind her. Together the pair flung themselves headlong into the ore-filled cargo wagon, Jess slamming the door shut again, Sal swooping in to shoot its interior bolt.

Jess's head spun as she scanned the freight car, the lightstick she'd looped around her neck illuminating their all-steel surroundings. There were no windows here, of course, which was good. And, as far as Jess could see, no gaps in any of the doors either. At least, none that were big enough for those things to get through. Also good.

For now anyway, it seemed they were safe.

Apparently of the same opinion, Sally let out a sigh and sagged to the floor of the car, her back propped against the door she'd just bolted.

Jess slumped down beside her.

"Okay then," Sal said eventually, "so... train-eating monster, flesh-stripping acid, blood-sucking worm things. Think we're quite done piling on the 'ol jeopardy here?" upon which regrettable words the cargo wagon gave a sudden violent lurch, its walls, its floor, its roof, all crumpling inwards several centimeters at once, as if the entire car were being crushed slowly in some titanic junkyard masher.

Huddled against the freight car's end door, Sally just let her head drop onto her knees. "I know, I *know,*" she said to Jess, "sometimes I really should just keep my big mouth shut."

15

Chunky is the Enemy

Crowds were gathering, Vera noted with rising concern. Gathering quickly too. Already, a nervous, murmuring audience of a hundred or more had assembled, not even half an hour on from... from... Vera could still barely bring herself to think about it. About what had happened. Even now it felt entirely unreal— *sur*real—like a twisted joke in some nightmarish version of one of those old cartoons they showed before the main feature at Jolly's.

"My god! Would ya look at the *size* of that thing!" she heard someone in the crowd say, which just made her want to turn and yell at them all—

to tell them to go home, get the hell gone, nothing to see here that wasn't ripping Vera apart inside.

In the end though, she bit her tongue. Because who could blame them really? It was, Vera knew, almost unheard of to see a trillopax out in the open like this, let alone involved in the kind of dramatic scene of which this creature was currently the gargantuan star. Such being the case, onlookers— and *lots* of them—had been an inevitability from the moment news of 'the incident' had reached the surrounding settlement. Most were respectfully quiet at least, conscious, Vera presumed, of the situation's desperate life and death stakes.

Yeah, right, Vera's darker half put in. *You really think Sally and Jess are still* alive *in there? Cos you saw that thing's mouth slam shut, right? You saw how it—*

Vera swayed where she stood, horror twisting at her guts. Suddenly it was all she could do not to throw up on the spot. Which, right at this moment, would have been a *very* bad idea, seeing as how she was encased head-to-toe in a full-body hazmat suit, including close-fitting face-mask.

Hauling in a deep breath, Vera straightened and forced herself to glance over at the trillopax, still on the railtrack where it had come to rest after eating the train (and Sally, and Jess...). Apart from an ongoing series of rippling gulps that traversed the creature's preposterous length with a sound like the galaxy's biggest garbage crusher, the trillopax had barely moved at all in the last half hour. Apparently, after a feast of such richness and abundance, your average, unfeasibly gigantic, genetically-engineered-for-the-mining-industry centipede monster needed a good lie down. Once again, who could blame it, Vera supposed.

"Okay, that's you, ma'am," the technician behind Vera said as he completed his final checks on the hazmat suit.

"You too, sir. All good," a second technician said to Isaac Lovelight, the little vet standing shoulder to shoulder with Vera in an almost identical full-body hazmat.

Vera nodded, glad that, if nothing else, the tech-team were happy. Because someone *else* certainly wasn't. *Dave,* to name names. As he had been doing ever since they'd hatched this outlandish rescue plan, the boy from Staines paced back and forth just a little way off, chewing a nail and dividing his time between furious glances at the sleeping trillopax and skeptical ones at Vera and Isaac. Truth be told, and continuing a theme, one could hardly blame *him* either, Vera thought. As far as rescue plans went, 'outlandish' barely covered the facts in the case of this current effort. Couple that with Dave's unexpressed but clearly growing feelings for Jess (not to mention Vera's own similarly unexpressed ones for Sally), and, well, let's just say that emotions had every cause to run high here.

As Vera and Isaac thanked their respective tech-people, the squeal of skidding tires cut across the exchange, and all four of them spun to see a rusty old jeep come screeching to a halt just meters away. At the jeep's wheel was a grim-faced Declan, and the spray of gravel from the vehicle's juddering stop had barely rattled to earth again before the Irishman leapt from the driver's seat, hauled something from the jeep's rear, and sprinted up to Vera and Isaac with it.

The something in question was a black leather case, the kind a doctor (or indeed a vet) might carry on professional visits.

"You sure that's got all you need in it?" Declan said to Isaac as he dumped the case at the vet's feet.

"Oh, my love," Isaac replied, opening the bag to inspect its contents, "you would be *amazed* at what I manage to pack in here."

The remark, innocuous though it surely was, turned out to be something of a last straw for Dave, who promptly ceased his anxious pacing, fixed his most skeptical look yet on the assembled group, and blurted, "Okay, look, this is freakin nuts! You are seriously going *into* that thing? Let's just *kill* it! We can cut it open with the Cannonball's laser, get Jess and Sally out that way. We can——"

Isaac shook his head. "Not a good idea, lovely,

believe me."

"Why not?"

"Ever been fishing? Seen a worm when you stick a hook through it? The death throes of our somewhat larger friend here would crush every last thing inside it to scrap before we got anywhere near your two trapped friends. Please, just trust me on this."

Dave opened his mouth as if to object again but was cut off by a sudden, ear-splitting hiss, and together the group turned to see the Cannonball Express edging its way backwards down the track the trillopax lay asleep on. As had been the case since last night's theft, only four of Trans-Mars Haulage's wagons—coal tender, crew car, passenger car, empty flatbed—remained hitched to the loco, but while Vera and the others stood watching the train reverse, the rear of its flatbed closed in on a *fifth* piece of rolling stock, waiting there on the track. This wagon was of a type Vera had never seen before and bore a huge reel of metal cabling mounted on what looked like some kind of motorized winch mechanism.

Directing these proceedings trackside was the woman called Sara Winchester, the mining company's boss, while at the Cannonball's throttle, peering behind him out a side window, was one of her employees—perhaps the man who had driven the diesel last night, Vera speculated.

Murmurs of anticipation rippled through the crowd as the rear coupling on the empty flatbed clanked into the corresponding coupling on the winch wagon, following which, Sara darted forward to fix the locking pin, securing the winch wagon to the rest of the train.

"What the *hell* is she doing?" a scowling Declan growled.

A very good question, Vera thought. The plan they'd all agreed on half an hour ago was to send Isaac and Vera into the trillopax with two spare hazmat suits for Sally and Jess, then simply escort the trapped pair out again before the creature had awoken from its post-lunch nap. Winch wagons and the Cannonball? Neither had been *any part* of that plan.

As Declan hurried away to confront Sara, another technician stepped up to Vera clutching the end of some narrow plastic tubing. Vera recognized the flexible corrugated pipe straightaway as that used in voice-tube installations, and she raised her arms to let the technician clip the end of the pipe to the sturdy leather harness Vera wore over her hazmat suit. The rest of the acoustic tubing stretched back from Vera to a separate free-standing spool-housing, around which the bulk of the tubing remained coiled, and from whose center there sprouted a large brass voice-tube horn. Maintaining some

112

kind of contact with the outside world once they were in the trillopax would, everyone had agreed, be crucial for Vera and Isaac, and primitive though it might be, a standalone voice-tube system was the best—really the *only*—option for achieving that. Not for the first time since moving to Mars, Vera found herself lamenting the way in which all electronics—be they complex computer systems or simple walkie-talkie radios—were rendered useless by the planet's tempestuous, EMP-riddled atmosphere, itself a perpetual and unavoidable side-effect of the ongoing terraforming process. Even now, dense clouds of gunmetal gray were once again gathering above, the rumble of storms distant and not-so-distant stirring the early afternoon air. Hey, as they said, ho…

Beside Vera, Isaac Lovelight dropped suddenly to his knees, before which, laid out on the dusty ground, were two canvas shoulder bags. Both bags already contained a spare hazmat suit—one each for Sally and Jess—and Isaac began now to fill the remaining space in the bags with items from his black leather vet's case. As the fellow worked, Vera found her eyes drawn once more to the near impossible horror that was the sleeping trillopax…

"Handsome chap, don't you think?" Isaac said. "If Valentino were a monster centipede whose digestive system could metabolize uranium… et voilà!"

Vera did her best to smile back, but right now her best was nowhere near good enough. Instead, she drew in a slow steadying breath and, emotions thusly marshalled, cocked a curious head at Isaac Lovelight. "So... have you ever... you know... done anything like this before?"

"Like this? Oh lordy, my lovely, no! This is complete insanity."

Once again, the man's attempt at levity bombed, Vera returning only a gape of shock, and with his face falling in regret, Isaac reached out to lay a supportive hand on Vera's shoulder. "But it *will* work," he said to her. "I swear."

Vera did manage a smile this time. Even followed through with a firm(-ish) nod, her respect—her *affection* even—for the oddball veterinarian growing just a little more. The fellow was, after all, putting his own life at serious risk here, and for two people he hadn't even met.

"I *am* sorry, you know," Vera said to him. "For earlier. For... *threatening* you..."

"No, you're not," the little man replied. "And neither should you be. *I'm* the one who ought to apologize to *you*. Now come on, my love, let's get these bags packed."

As Vera set to helping Isaac stock the shoulder bags they would take into the trillopax, the sound of Declan and Sara's raised voices drifted over from the Cannonball, the pair evidently at significant loggerheads as they stood arguing by the loco's newly hitched winch wagon:

"To hell with the *cargo,*" Declan was saying. "This isn't *about* the cargo! We need to——"

"Look, I *understand,*" Sara interrupted, "I *do,* and your friends *are* our priority here. But we absolutely *need* to retrieve that uranium too. Please, trust me here," and grabbing the hooked end of the winch wagon's cable, Sara began to march towards Isaac and Vera, the braided steel line unspooling behind her as she pulled it along.

Clearly far from mollified, Declan was just setting off after Sara when another massive gulp-like ripple traveled the length of the trillopax, the muffled sound of grinding metal from inside the monster echoing across the sprawling mine complex. Vera felt her knotted stomach twist tighter still, and the crowd murmured its own escalating fear.

Sara, though, simply carried on regardless. "Isaac, a word," she said as she stepped up to the vet and attached the winch wagon cable's hooked end to Isaac's leather harness.

Stuffing some final supplies into the two shoulder bags he and Vera knelt before, Isaac climbed to his feet, grabbed the bag nearest him, and headed off with Sara for the trillopax, more of the winch wagon cable unspooling behind them as they went. Sara bent Isaac's ear as the pair moved away, but her words were too low for Vera to hear now.

After another moment, Declan, still manifestly unhappy with the mine boss, rejoined Vera and Dave, and once Vera had slung her own bag over her shoulder, all three of them began to head for the trillopax too, the voice-tube piping Vera was attached to unspooling behind her from its standalone reel-mount.

As they drew nearer to the sleeping creature, Declan must have spotted the growing fear in Vera's face. "Okay, look," he said to her, "if you think you're not gonna be able to do this, that's not an issue. Seriously. I could take over and——"

"I'm fine," Vera replied.

"Declan's right," Dave put in. "Just say the word and I'll do it instead. It's not——"

Isaac's voice rang out from up ahead: "That's enough from you two, my loves. Things are going to be *very* tight in there. *Petite* is our ally, remember? *Chunky* is the enemy," upon which final words they all came to a stop by the recumbent monster, the boys' brace of last-ditch objections trailing away into a petulant silence:

"Who's *chunky...*?"

"I'm big boned..."

Drawing in another steadying breath, Vera looked up at the creature before them. The head of the trillopax, surely thirty meters high from monstrous underjaw to ghastly ridge-topped skull plate, towered over the group like a mountain with teeth—a very *ugly* mountain with teeth— and once again Vera found herself struggling to beat back despair; to reject the awful conclusion that her two friends were most probably already...

But *no*.

No!

They *were* still alive in there. *Both* of them. Any other scenario was simply not worth considering, and corralling her terror for what must have been the third time in as many minutes, Vera forced herself to take a further measured look at the challenge they faced.

Although the mouth of the sleeping monster remained shut, there *was* a single dark opening in the nearly five-meter-high wall of its exposed teeth—an opening where the trillopax, as a result of declining health, had lost one of its forward incisors. Now, that same gap would prove neatly fortuitous, providing Vera and Isaac with a convenient way into the creature—a way that would not, they all hoped, disturb the animal unduly.

Vera felt someone take her hand and give it a squeeze. It was Isaac.

"Bit of Betsy, my love?" the vet said. "I think so.

Sing along now," and with a truly startling lack of self-consciousness, Isaac Lovelight launched full-throated into one of Betsy Bow's cornier classics. Even through his face mask, the fellow's bright and tuneful tenor rang out loud and clear as he took a determined step forward, gently pulling Vera along with him. "*Light a little candle in the darkest hour,*" he sang. "*Hurry ol' man trouble on his way...*"

Just five steps later, on the threshold of the tooth gap itself, they both paused for a moment, and while the very rankest of odors rolled out at them from the darkness beyond that rotting gumline, Isaac reached up to the mask of his hazmat suit and ignited the twin gas lamps there. This done, he released Vera's hand, smiled at her, and then climbed up through the tooth opening, pulling behind him the unspooling cable from the winch wagon. "*Dance a little quickstep in that April shower,*" the vet sang as he vanished into the dark, "*and serenade those stubborn skies of gray...*"

Drawing in one last deep breath, Vera gathered the scant remains of her faltering courage, ignited the lamps on her own mask, and followed, the voice-tube piping that was clipped to her harness continuing to uncoil from its standalone reel-mount behind.

Within seconds, and in brute defiance of her suit's integrated lighting-system, the brightness of the Martian daytime was replaced almost entirely by a gloom so stagnant, so oppressive, Vera all but felt it as a physical dead weight, compressing her chest, dragging at her limbs. At the same time, the *smell* that had seemed so nauseating from outside the creature soared to appalling new heights— heights that once again had Vera battling the urge to vomit into her face mask.

And all the while, from up ahead, Isaac's sweet, melodic voice continued to ring out, echoing through the darkness:

> "Sunbeams warm and bright
> Will turn the night to day,
> So light a little candle in the darkest hour
> And hurry ol' man trouble on his way..."

16

Belly of the Beast

In the yellow-green glow of the lightstick looped around her neck, Jess paced and re-paced the width of the freight car's interior. Paced it in a sullen, clench-jawed fury. Because dammit, there had to be a way out of this. Just *had* to. So far though, Jess's ongoing study of the car's all-steel interior, as well as its limited and entirely unhelpful contents (twenty-three drums of uranium ore), had yielded precisely nothing in the nature of a realistic escape plan.

Worse still, time was *not* their friend here. Since that initial echoing slam of the trillopax's massive jaws, Jess had counted an even dozen individual convulsions of the monster's gut—roughly one every two minutes—each instance crushing the car they were trapped in just a little bit more and sending it a few centimeters deeper down the creature's digestive tract. Around Jess and Sally, the car's interior volume had already shrunk by at least twenty percent, metal panelwork buckling inwards in angular folds of rusted steel, welded seams threatening at any moment to split and allow those intestinal parasite creatures to come flooding in. And as if all that weren't enough, there was the acid too. At the other, *lower* end of the now sloping wagon, the sizzling pool of digestive fluid continued to grow, its frothing edge creeping ever closer to Jess and Sal's end of the wagon as the corrosive liquid oozed in through whatever cracks it had managed to find in the crumpling truck.

"Okay," Jess said at last, shaking her head in something that was now perilously close to despair, "way I see it, there's gonna be no space *outside* the train—*between* the train exterior and the gut wall, I mean—for us to squeeze ourselves out that way, agreed?"

"Agreed," Sally said, the gal crouched unhappily in a corner, glaring upwards as if she hoped somehow to evolve laser eye-beams and blast her way out through the ceiling.

"And even if there *were* some space there," Jess

continued, "there's the *acid* to consider as well."

"Uh-huh."

"Not to mention those spiked worm things."

"Let's call 'em *spurms*."

Jess gave the remark the sardonic eyebrow-raise it deserved, Sally returning a frustrated sigh:

"Look, just find me something to punch and I'll stop saying stupid crap, okay?" following which, and for lack of anything more yielding and bad-guy-shaped to hand, the gal proceeded once again to pound a fist into a nearby steel wall panel.

With a shoulder-sagging sigh of her own, Jess turned to ponder for the fourth, maybe the *fifth* time the wagon's bolted end door—the one she and Sal had entered through. "So, like it or not, our best bet is still, *somehow* or other, back the way we came. Up through the center of the train and then hopefully out the loco's forward window."

"Uh-huh. And what about the... ah, damn it, too late, now they're *spurms*. What about the spurms *inside* the train? Between here and the loco?"

Jess sagged again. "Gaaaaah, I dunno. Maybe they've all... moved *on* now or... or something," and taking a couple of steps towards the car's end door, Jess carefully unbolted it, pulled the heavy steel panel open just the tiniest crack—

—and the heads of a dozen or more parasites came surging through in a squirming, wriggling rush of pallid flesh and acid-dripping spines.

Jess slammed the door shut again, decapitating several of the invading creatures and forcing the rest of them back outside.

Slumping into the corner with Sally, Jess finally gave in to the defeated groan she'd been stifling for the last half-hour. "Okay, I admit it. I am drawing blanks here. Currently I have no earthly idea how we are gonna—"

"Sally! Jess! Are you there?"

Startled rigid, Jess and Sal exchanged twin looks of astonishment and whirled to where the voice—where *Vera's* voice—had come from—

—which turned out to be the voice-tube unit installed by the freight car's end door. As one, Jess and Sally leapt for the small brass box, Jess getting there first and barking into its miniature horn:

"Vera? Vera, is that you?"

● ● ●

Huddled in the driver's compartment of the diesel, her hazmat suit's gas lamps playing over the cramped and disintegrating interior, Vera gave a stunned gasp and jammed the handset of the cab's extendible voice-tube hard into the surface of her face mask. "Oh golly, thank god!" she blurted. "Yes, it's me! Jess, are you okay? Please tell me you're okay."

"Relax, Vera. I'm okay," Jess's voice came back

over the voice-tube.

"And… and Sally?" Vera said, her guts churning, her throat desert dry. "Is she——"

"Chipper, babe," came Sally's voice now too. "All the better for hearing your dulcet tones."

Releasing the mother of all sighs, Vera sagged against a wall and allowed herself the briefest of inward smiles—*Dulcet tones!*—before hauling her focus back onto the less-than-rosy-hued here and now. "All right," she said, "so where *are* you both?"

"Where are *we?*" an incredulous Jess answered. "Where are *you,* girl? How in hell are we even *talking* here? How'd you find us?"

"Tell you later, but we've just made it to the locomotive. We're coming to get you."

"Wait. *This* train's locomotive? The *diesel?*"

"Yes, we're——"

"Oh god, Vera, you have to be careful. There's these creatures——"

"Spurms," Sally's voice chipped in.

"… *Excuse* me?" Vera replied.

"Kind of spiked worm things," Jess clarified.

"Ah, yes, we know," Vera said. "We've met them already. Lovely, aren't they? But it's all right. We're in special hazmat suits. Apparently not very tasty to the little buggers, pardon my français," with which words Vera shot a look through the cab's broken forward window to where Isaac, crouched at the front of the train on

124

a pulsing hump of intestinal muscle, was in the process of completing the task Sara had assigned him, namely: attaching the hooked end of the winch wagon cable—*titanium,* apparently, not steel—to the forward coupling on the diesel. All around the little vet, worm parasites in their thousands continued to swarm, but for now at least, the creatures seemed to be steering clear of the man himself. Whatever the techies had impregnated the hazmat suits with, it certainly seemed to be working.

"Cool," Sally's voice piped up again through the voice-tube. "Though I gotta say, gal, your français? 'Bout the lamest I heard outside of a Mormon kindergarten. You ever decide you wanna learn how to curse like a pro, you come see ol' Sal, know what I'm saying?"

Despite her strenuous efforts to remain focused, Vera felt her inner smile broaden.

"Anyways," Sally continued, "ya got a couple of them thar hazmats for the babes in the wood here?"

"Yes, we do," Vera confirmed, just as a puffing Isaac Lovelight, his task complete, clambered back in through the diesel's forward window and dropped to the floor of the cab.

"Okay, great," Jess said. "And delighted to confirm that we're not actually that far from you. Just three carriages down. If you head on through the train till you get to the—"

"Ah," Vera interrupted. "I'm sorry, Jess, but I'm afraid it's not going to be quite that easy."

"Tell me."

Vera shot a glance through the rear door of the diesel's cab, her heart sinking yet again at the sight that greeted her eyes. Because the access passage beyond that door—the one that led *through* the diesel and out the back of the locomotive—was crushed almost beyond recognition, a canted mass of crumpled and buckled metal, impassable to anything larger than one of those spiked worm monstrosities they all held so dear. In terms of the rescue plan, this had left Vera and Isaac with just one feasible course of action. "We're going to have to squeeze our way down the *outside* of the train to get to you," Vera explained. "And then get *all* of us back out again the same way."

Jess's response was immediate and edged with fear: "Nuh-uh. Vera, that's not gonna work. This thing is *crushing* us on *all sides*. There *is* no space to get down the outside of the train."

From the corner of an eye, Vera saw Isaac open his shoulder bag and pull from it a large, drug-loaded syringe, the vet's chirpy musical-theater tenor ringing out once more: "*Sunbeams warm and bright will turn the night to day...*"

"It's okay, Jess," Vera said, "apparently we've got that covered too," and no sooner had Isaac reached through the cab's shattered side window, jabbed the syringe into the wall of intestinal muscle there, and depressed the plunger, than Vera saw that same wall of muscle begin to relax, receding several centimeters at once from the loco's flank. Isaac turned to Vera, gave her a smiling thumbs-up, then set about climbing out through the side window, inserting his slender frame into the space left by the receding expanse of flesh. "*So light a little candle in the darkest hour,*" the vet sang, "*and hurry ol' man trouble on his way...*"

"I'm going to have to go now," Vera said to Jess through the voice-tube, "but I'm hooking you up to the others, okay? To the outside," and seizing the acoustic piping she'd dragged with her into the trillopax, Vera plugged the pipe's end fitting into an auxiliary input on the diesel's voice-tube system. "Dave, Declan," she called into the handset, "are you there? Can you hear me?"

Dave's response was instant—"Whoah! Yeah! Loud and clear!"—and was followed immediately by another from Declan, the Irishman's voice tight with anxiety:

"What about Jess and Sally? Are they—"

"Alive and kicking," Jess herself chimed in before Vera could answer.

"Though, if I'm honest, more *actual* kicking might be nice," Sally added, and as the sound of the boys' relieved sighs echoed over the voice-tube, Vera finally allowed herself a smile of the outward variety. Because yes, so far, everything seemed to be going more or less according to plan. Maybe this crazy rescue attempt of theirs really *would* work after all.

"You two ladies just stay exactly where you are then," Vera said into the voice-tube.

"Oh, believe me, sweetie," Sally replied, "right now we are going nowhere."

Sweetie...

Forcing herself yet again to refocus, Vera turned to the side window and watched Isaac, now fully outside the diesel once more, select another section of gut flesh farther down the loco then plunge a second syringe into it. As before, the muscle receded almost instantly, and the little vet went on to squeeze himself into the space created, edging several more centimeters down the trillopax's digestive tract, towards the rear of the train. Just as he was about to disappear from view beyond the edge of the window frame, he raised his eyes to Vera, shot her a final cheery smile, then moments later, even as he was pulling a third syringe from his shoulder bag, the man was gone.

Vera drew in a slow, steadying breath, released it again, and pressed the handset of the voice-tube to her face mask: "Okay," she said, "so just you hang in there, gals. Because we are on our way."

"Good to know," Jess replied. "Take care, hon," following which Vera placed the voice-tube's handset back on its cradle, reached into her shoulder bag, and was just pulling out a syringe of her own when the cab suddenly rocked with its most brutal lurch yet. Thrown violently from her feet to go crashing into the wall panel opposite, Vera choked back a scream, dropped into the nearest corner for safety, and felt the loco—felt the entire *train*—slip a few centimeters farther down the trillopax's convulsing gut.

"Um, and Vera..." came Jess's voice again over the voice-tube.

Heart throttling up into overdrive, Vera watched as, all around her, the walls and floor and ceiling of the diesel's cab crumpled inwards at least another five centimeters...

"I know, Jess," she breathed. "I know..."

17

Worst. Pajama Party. Ever.

Jess had been sure, *dead* sure, that the trillopax's last titanic gut convulsion—the one whose concluding tremors still rattled the crumpling steel walls of the freight car—would be the one finally to split its welded seams and bring on an icky, spurmy end for fifty percent of Trans-Mars Haulage's ragtag yet loveable crew. But no. Apparently the ancient piece of rolling stock they were trapped inside, buckled and twisted though it was, still had some fight left in it, and as the creature's digestive spasms faded again into stillness, Jess and Sally breathed a mutual sigh of relief, before sagging back into their seated positions against the car's end door.

Thereafter, a relative quiet fell in the green-tinged and foul-smelling gloom.

"So," Sally said eventually, brushing fallen rust flakes and spilt uranium ore powder from the tattered remains of her babydoll, "acid levels rising, walls closing in, giant intestinal parasites out for blood. Seriously, babe. Worst. Pajama party. Ever."

Jess glanced down at her own ravaged nightwear and, despite everything, somehow managed a smile. "You wanna braid each other's hair? Swap makeup tips?"

"Makeup tips? From *you?* Babe, I'd sooner get 'em from the giant intestinal parasites."

Funny? Yeah, maybe, Jess conceded, but in all honesty, a little too near the knuckle to prompt anything more than a wry grimace from her right now. "Well, gee, thanks, Sal," Jess said. "Not like I'm *already* soiling my scanties about this frickin *date* tonight. If, of course, there even *is* a date tonight. Cos hey, at this rate——"

"Whoah, just you stop right there, Ms. Glass-Half-Empty! Forget ye not, we have got Captain Finishing School and the Fanboy Kid on the case here. Seriously, if *that* pair can't devise and implement a daring and spectacular rescue plan, then I ask you, who can? Also, be heartily obliged if you chose *not* to answer that. File under rhetorical, if you get my drift."

Another reluctant smile from Jess.

"And hey, as for *tonight*," Sally continued, "girl, what is your problem? *You* are gonna *ace* it, babe. Big Blonde and Irish? Dude is *clearly* into you. And I mean *super* clearly. He——"

Alarm flared in Jess's chest as she suddenly remembered the door-mounted voice-tube unit and *who* might be listening on the other end of it. Reaching up, Jess slammed an open palm over the unit's miniature horn, simultaneously flashing her eyes at Sal to encourage some shutting-the-hell-up. Or, if such proved impossible (often the case with Sal), at least some dialing-it-down-a-notch so that the 'dude' in question might not hear.

Thankfully, Sally *did* keep the rest of it down, though Jess maintained a firm hand over the voice-tube's horn anyway, just to be safe.

"Seriously, babe," Sal whispered, shaking her head in a kind of mystified wonder, "it's like you never even been on a date before."

The remark, casually intended though it clearly was, took Jess somewhat by surprise, and despite her every intention of offering a similarly casual reply, what followed instead was, well… silence.

Lots of silence.

Endless, tumbleweed-strewn *acres* of silence.

Eventually, Sally's jaw fell open. "Oh my *god*," she said, "you have *never* even been on a *date* before?"

Praying that Declan really couldn't hear any of this through the hand she continued to hold over the voice-tube horn, Jess once again struggled to find a suitable response and in the end came back with—yes, you guessed it, folks—a whole bunch *more* silence.

"Are you frickin *serious?*" Sally went on, jaw slackening still further.

Normal service had a lackluster stab at resuming: "Well... um... ah... I... um... *did* once take off my bra for Josh Baxter."

"... Yeah? And?"

"And... made us a couple of sweet catapults outta the elastic. Bulls-eyed every last rat in Josh's dad's barn. *Damn,* that was a good day."

Needless to say, this charming but unhelpful anecdote did little to arrest the southward trajectory of Sally's jaw, or extinguish the ever merrier glint in the gal's evil frickin eyes.

"Oh, come *on,* Sal," Jess whisper-blurted (if that wasn't a thing before, it was now), "it's *me.* Guys see me, they don't wanna *date* me, they want me to flush their carburetors or grease their pistons, and *yes,* I am *well aware* of the innuendo, thank you very much, and *now,* cos of your great big yackety-yack mouth, I have gotta go out on an *actual date* tonight, somehow *not* looking like I wrestle in engine oil for a living!"

133

"Hey hey hey, babe, *relax*," Sally whispered back. "I get it. I do. Something like this? It's a big deal for a gal. I understand that. It was for me too, you know, back in the day."

"What, when you were *eight?*"

"Oh, please, *six*. What can I say? You kick the bully's ass in kindergarten, you acquire admirers."

None of this was helping matters, Jess felt, and she endeavored to communicate as much to Sally through the time-honored medium of sulking.

"Okay, look," Sally said, apparently getting the message and adopting a more conciliatory tone, "don't worry, okay? I mean it. Because I, Sally Chu, Master of Mascara, Wielder of the Lipgloss that Conquered the World, have *totally* got your back here, know what I'm saying?"

Jess considered for a long moment, before huffing out a reluctant sigh and nodding.

"Your *front*, on the other hand... well *that* is a *complete* lost cause."

Jess glowered.

"Joke. *Bad* joke. Not the time for comedy. Received and understood. But look, I *swear* to you, girl, come seven o'clock this evening, *you* are gonna look like a frickin *goddess*. Cuter than Pickford, classier than Garbo. The boy will gasp. I promise you, babe. *Gasp*," upon which steadfast declaration Sally raised her right hand to the high-five position while simultaneously fixing Jess with her most thoroughly bad-ass, *honey-we-have-got-this* look.

And damn, but who could fail to respond to that, right? Certainly not Jess. Removing her hand from the voice-tube horn, she smiled back at her friend and high-fived her hard, the sound of their impacting palms echoing through the truck.

A brief silence followed.

Emphasis on the *brief,* of course, seeing as how Sally still hadn't gone anywhere.

"Seriously though," the gal murmured with a grin, "your *first date?*"

"Well hey," Jess hissed back, "forgive me if everything with a pulse doesn't just fall at my hot Asian feet wherever I tread," following which riposte, and to Jess's complete surprise, Sally's grin promptly sloughed from her face like suds down a shower curtain, to be replaced by a petulant and most uncharacteristic pout.

"Yeah, well… not *everything,*" the gal mumbled.

At first, Jess was at a loss to understand Sally's abrupt descent into glumness, but then a second later it clicked. "Oh, come on, *really? This* again? Vera does not *hate* you, Sal."

"Uh-huh," Sally muttered, picking imaginary debris from her babydoll and looking anywhere but at Jess.

"So if you care that much, why don't you—"

"Okay, once again, I do not *care*," Sally snapped,

anger flashing into her eyes even as she refused still to meet Jess's probing gaze. "Like I said before, it's the *principle*."

Jess was on the point of expressing further incredulity at Sally's frankly mystifying attitude when something in the gal's reaction—something profoundly at odds with the Sally they all knew and loved—prompted Jess to take a mental timeout instead. For a moment or two more, Jess sat there in pensive silence, studying the inexplicably petulant/glum/angry face of her best friend, scrutinizing those perfect pin-up gal features at a forensic level, until at last:

"*Oh...* Oh my god, you *care!* You *totally care!* You *like* Vera!"

Sally's eyes shot wide, finally whirling Jess's way again and beaming out a zillion watts of *dammit-I-am-totally-busted.* "What? No. I... *what?*" the gal blustered. "No, that ain't it at all. I—"

"*Un*believable," Jess plowed on, reveling, she would freely admit, in the sheer unexpected delight of the moment. Because seriously, to catch Sally 'I Totally Got This' Chu on the back foot *at all*, in *any* kind of situation, was the very rarest of rare things. But to do it in a situation like this one right here? A situation with such *potential...*

"Vera *Middleton?*" Jess blurted with epic glee.

"Hey, *enough!* I do *not*—"

"*Our Vera* has breached the blast-proof,

titanium-reinforced heart of *Sally Chu?*"

Sally opened her mouth as if to object again but seemed to think better of it and instead just flung her head back against the steel door with a resounding CLANG. "Okay, *yes!*" the gal growled, throwing up her hands in defeat. "Happy now? *Yes!* So I find myself mystifyingly attracted to the super-hot British gal with the perfect skin and the voice like frickin maple syrup. I swear though, Jessica Flint, you say *one word* to her, and you are dead meat. I mean it, babe..."

● ● ●

"... Vera *cannot* know this. She ever finds out that I got... got..."

"Feelings?"

"... the *hots* for her, I swear to god, I am moving to Neptune."

The words, every impossible bewildering one of them, emerged from the voice-tube unit by the side door of the train's crew car. Emerged clear as crystal in the surrounding silence. And outside that same door, raised syringe forgotten in her hand as she stood listening through a broken window, Vera Middleton all at once found herself the very definition of agog.

18

Getting a Little Hot

Someone else was speaking, Vera realized.

Someone *not* on the voice-tube.

Someone *not* Sally...

Isaac, of course. That was his name.

"Something wrong, my love?" the fellow called over to Vera, the pair of them now halfway down the exterior of the crew car, Vera on one side of it, Isaac the other. "Still with us?"

Words. Yes. That's what they were. Vera remembered words. Little things. Made of letters. You strung them together to make sentences. Well, in theory at least. Because at this precise moment, as Vera stood there gawping at the now silent door-mounted voice-tube—the one from whose tiny brass horn Sally's inconceivable declaration had issued not ten seconds ago—the exact method by which one strung together these 'word' objects to form these so-called 'sentences' appeared to have deserted Vera entirely. Behind her hazmat suit's mask, her jaw moved up and down, her tongue made every effort to support the cause, but there, for now, the process stalled.

"Vera, my love," Isaac Lovelight persisted, "a simple nod will suffice."

At last, Vera looked up and met Isaac's eyes, peering at the fellow through broken windows, across the width of the half-crushed crew car between them. But before she could muster a coherent response, another voice completely emerged from the voice-tube:

"Vera, Isaac," Declan said, "if either of you is somewhere you can hear this, there are two not remotely chunky guys out here who would appreciate a progress report."

Hopeful that the power of speech would return through determined effort, Vera opened her mouth to answer Declan... but then closed it again. Because of course, any reply from Vera on the voice-tube would surely alert Sally to the fact that Vera had been within earshot during Sally's shocking (and glorious, and beautiful, and utterly *utterly* preposterous) confession. And somehow, having Sally *know* that Vera had *heard* that confession; having Sally *know* that Vera *knew*...

By this point, an increasingly confused Isaac Lovelight was staring hard from across the carriage, motioning for Vera to respond to Declan's request. The voice-tube horn *was*, after all, on *her* side of the car, Isaac himself a good four meters from it. Thankfully however, following some frantic if obscure hand-flapping from Vera, the vet, while clearly still confused, seemed to get the general message and at last came through with a response of his own:

"Um, I'm here, lovely," Isaac said to Declan, bellowing through the broken windows from the carriage's other side. "So far, so good. We're about halfway down the outside of the crew car now. The interior is still pretty well impassible, but the muscle relaxant seems to be working well. At this rate we'll reach your friends in about ten minutes. And once we've got them out, we might have the whole train free an hour after that."

"Okay, sounds good," Declan said. "How's the temperature in there?"

Vera saw Isaac's eyes dart to the condensation dripping down the inside of his hazmat mask, and Vera's own eyes followed suit, the condensation inside *her* mask not quite so bad but significant nonetheless.

"Getting a little hot, now you mention it," Isaac

replied. "Why?"

• • •

Poised with Dave by the freestanding voice-tube system, Declan knew that what he was about to say would not go down well with Doctor Isaac Lovelight. Nope, not at *all* well. But keeping such crucial intel from the troops at the front was simply not an option here, so taking a deep breath, Declan sought to summarize the situation in as measured a voice as he could muster:

"It looks as if the creature has begun to metabolize the uranium ore in the train's rearmost wagons."

"Ah," Lovelight's voice came back. "Well, *that's* not good."

No, it was not, Declan knew, and turning again to survey the slumbering trillopax, he noted with a surge of dismay that the clouds of vapor rising from the creature's rear half seemed to have doubled in volume since the last time he'd checked. Possibly even *tripled*. Declan clearly wasn't the only one alarmed by this increasingly rapid escalation either. On the periphery of the bizarre scene, the still gathering crowds stood muttering their own growing fear, watching ever-more-wide-eyed as a frowning Sara Winchester pressed a complex-looking measuring device to the monster's steaming hide.

And through it all, over by the trillopax's head end, it stood there still—the gleaming red and gold bulk of the Cannonball Express, the winch wagon that had been hitched to its rear no longer spooling out cable now that Lovelight had hooked the end of that cable to the loco trapped in the trillopax's belly...

Crazy. Absolutely crazy, Declan thought yet again, still unable to believe what Sara planned to attempt once Jess and Sally were clear of the trillopax. Using the Cannonball to extract the entire train? Cargo and all? To Declan it seemed like utter folly. Even more so now the creature had begun to metabolize the uranium. Because how much longer did they even have before it got too hot in there to do anything at all?

"You're absolutely right, Doctor Lovelight," Declan said, leaning in to the voice-tube horn. "*Good* it most certainly is not. Time is of the essence here. We need to—"

"No."

The interruption, gruff and commanding, came from Sara, the woman appearing without warning at Declan's shoulder. "I am truly sorry, people," she said, "but time just ran out."

At Declan's other shoulder, Dave scowled, his voice tight with fear. "What do you mean?"

Presenting the device she'd been pressing to the trillopax's hide—essentially just a fancy

142

thermometer, Declan knew—Sara showed them the instrument's readings. "At the rate the trillopax's temperature is rising, everyone inside it will be unconscious in around ten minutes. At *most*. We need to get that train out of there, and we need to do it *now*."

Declan felt his already twisted guts knot tighter still. "No," he said. "No way. Vera and your Lovelight fella, they haven't even made it to the first cargo wagon yet. Most of the train is still gonna be wedged tight."

"Doesn't matter," Sara insisted, "we have to try. Trust me, we do *not* have a choice here," with which the woman shoved Declan and Dave aside and all but thrust her head into the voice-tube's brass horn. "Okay everybody, wherever the hell you are, get yourselves *inside* that train *right now*." Then, to Declan and Dave: "You two, *go!* You know what to do."

For a second, Declan considered voicing further objections, but the look in Sara's eyes told him they were beyond that now—*way* beyond— and turning on his heels he took off with Dave, the pair of them racing full-pelt for the Cannonball.

●●●

Heart pounding, Vera wrenched open the side door of the crew car and squeezed her way into the wrecked and twisted carriage. Opposite her,

Isaac did the same via a broken window on the carriage's other side. Protruding glass shards in the window frame tore long gashes in the vet's hazmat suit as he forced his way through, but eventually the man stumbled up to Vera and grabbed her hand in support as the two of them hunkered down in the aisle.

•••

In Cargo Wagon Number One, Jess had barely finished processing the dark implications in Sara Winchester's words when the woman herself came through again on the voice-tube:

"And everybody, *hold on tight,* yes? This could get a little bumpy."

Spotting the dangling ends of some loose cargo straps above her, Jess rose to her feet and wound the heavy-duty webbing tight around both her wrists. Sally did the same.

"Okay," Jess yelled at the voice-tube unit, "ready when you are!"

•••

In the cab of the Cannonball, his neck craning out a side window, Declan saw Sara give the nod, and with a last anxious look to Dave beside him, he released the loco's brake. At the same time, poised by the engine's main controls, Dave wrenched a half dozen valves and levers in sequence, worked the throttle for several long seconds, and with an ear-pounding blast of steam and a screech of metal on metal, the Cannonball Express gave a single rattling lurch then started forward.

19

Stomach Upset

Heartrate skyrocketing, hands slick with sweat as they worked the throttle, Dave Hart tried not to think about Jess and Sally, trapped back there in god knew what kind of stomach-churning hell; tried instead to concentrate on the response of the loco at his command. That growling, hissing clatter as hundreds of tons of steam-driven Victorian tech set off down the track. Listening to the *voice* of the machinery you controlled was a crucial part of being a good engineer, Jess always said, and right now the voice from *this* piece of machinery was pretty damned definitive, roaring out a triumphant, *Let's do this, people! Let's fricking*

DO THIS!

But then, after just ten meters forward progress, the cable between winch wagon and monster suddenly drew taught, and the Cannonball lurched to a hard stop, its engine howling a cacophony of ear-splitting objections.

Through the cab windows, Dave saw the crowds reel, fear tightening their faces—

—while at the same time, and in the starkest of contrasts, the face of twenty-first century actor Warwick Davis beamed down at Dave from his soot-stained photo above the throttle. One of Dave's few mementos from his own time on twenty-first century Earth, the photo had become something of an unlikely talisman for the crew of the Cannonball, and reaching out now to touch its frame for luck, Dave murmured, "We have got this, Warwick. We have bloody *got* this…"

Jaw clenched, Dave opened the throttle a little more… only to recoil at the screech of steel on steel as the Cannonball's drive wheels lost traction, spinning uselessly on the rails beneath while friction sparks erupted in vast fiery fans.

Nothing. Not a single meter more did they travel, and Dave had just begun to throttle down again when all at once, from behind them, there came a sound that kicked Dave's already soaring terror into still higher orbit. It was the same sound they'd heard half an hour ago when they'd first approached the mining town—a monstrous, rumbling roar that drowned out completely the shriek of the Cannonball's engine. And as before, the sound turned out to be only the beginning of an even greater nightmare, because just as that colossal wall of noise reached its peak, the entire train jerked backwards, hauled with brutal ease back down the track for nearly a full five meters.

Heart lurching yet again, Dave shot another look through his side window and could only gasp in shock as he took in the mind-boggling sight of the trillopax to their rear, the vast creature now fully awake once more and squirming on the end of the titanium cable like a salmon on a fishing line.

•••

With the cargo straps biting deep into her wrists, Jess clung to the creaking steel sides of the rail wagon as it bucked and heaved around her. Next to Jess, Sally did the same, the pair of them slammed this way and that against the car's buckling metal wall panels.

At the other end of the truck, several ore drums broke free of their retaining straps, tumbling everywhere to smash against walls, floor, even the ceiling. Drum tops popped, and ore powder poured out, turning the deepening acid pool into a fizzing yellow mud that slushed around inside the jolting car, a liquid creature all its own, and one that threatened any second to lunge at Jess and Sally with its hissing, flesh-eating fingers.

But still the two of them held on, blood coursing down Jess's arms from where the cargo strapping tore at the skin of her wrists. And then, just seconds later, the wall panel directly opposite gave way entirely, Jess and Sally shrieking in mutual fright as, with a grinding metallic crunch, the massive sheet of corrugated steel buckled inwards nearly a full meter at once.

• • •

With every monstrous tug from the creature behind, the Cannonball was jerked farther and farther back down the track, and shaking with terror in the loco's cab, Dave whirled to Declan beside him:

"We need more traction!" he yelled to the Irishman, jabbing a forefinger at the lever that would steam-inject extra sand between the engine's drive wheels and the rails beneath.

But even as Declan rammed the lever home, the trillopax gave its most titanic thrash yet, this time rolling over completely and crashing down onto its back, multiple rows of centipede-like legs scrabbling at the dust-filled air.

• • •

In the crew car, Vera screamed with shock and

went crashing to the ceiling, now at her feet. She hit it hard, shoulder first, her scream morphing into a cry of pain even as Isaac came thudding down beside her. Struggling upright, Vera scanned the car in desperation, looking for something—*anything*—that the pair of them might cling to in this escalating and now upside-down madness.

•••

In the cargo wagon, upturned too and lurching more brutally than ever, Jess bit back the agony of what was surely a dislocated shoulder, she and Sally now suspended by their wrists from the cargo straps, feet flailing above a ceiling that had come to settle below. Opposite them, the collapsing main wall panel continued to buckle inwards, while directly beneath, the acid slush churned and splashed, an ocean of flesh-stripping death.

"Dammit, this is *not* gonna work!" Jess yelled to Sally. "We have got to—"

But a further screech of rupturing metal cut her short, and all at once Jess felt the wall panel she and Sal were lashed to start to buckle inwards as well, the two opposite sides of the crumpling cargo truck now closing in together like the jaws of some titanic vice.

20

Tug of War

No more than thirty seconds away from being crushed between the two collapsing sides of the freight wagon, Jess tore her eyes from the source of her imminent death and shot a desperate look at the wagon's end door—the one that led out to the crew car. Now situated above them in the upside-down truck, the door remained sealed, as it had done since Sally had bolted it shut to keep the parasite creatures out. But of course, that had been *then*. As things stood *now* however...

"Follow me," Jess yelled at Sally and, unlashing her wrists, began to climb the crumpling steel wall behind her, using the struts of the wagon's internal skeleton as foot- and hand-holds.

Clocking where Jess was headed, Sally's eyes widened in alarm. "Are you frickin kidding me? The spurms are still gonna be out there. Open that door and we're—"

But before Sally could finish, Jess hauled herself level with the door, yanked it open, and, on looking down, saw that, yes, there indeed were the worm parasites, squirming in their amassed thousands—

—but now stuck behind the steel wall panel that rose from the ceiling (currently below) to what would normally have been the top (but was now the bottom) of the doorframe. Not that the creatures would stay stuck there for long, Jess saw. Even as she watched, the things began to climb, surging against the upright metal panel in wave upon frenzied wave, all but forming a fleshy, squirming ramp to get to Jess above them.

"Okay, we got maybe ten seconds till those things make it up here," Jess yelled to Sally, who leapt into action at once, hauling herself clear of the encroaching wall panels and scaling the truck's skeletal substructure as Jess had. At the same time, Jess herself grabbed whatever she could find above and swung her body out through the end door, on into the space between the heaving freight wagon and the passenger car it was hitched to.

Seconds later, a gasping Sal joined her, clearing

the freight car doorway just as, with a dull crump, the car itself finally imploded, yellow acid slush gushing out through its end door to cascade onto the trillopax's pulsing gut flesh below.

Dangling with Sally from the coupling mechanism that connected the two inverted and lurching wagons, Jess risked another glance below and saw with a jolt of horror that the spurms were now less than a meter away, the things swarming up the end of the crushed cargo truck in an ever growing mountain, its probing, acid-slicked summit closing in on Jess and Sally's flailing feet.

Stifling a scream, Jess turned her eyes to the heavy steel coupler she and Sal hung from, reaching for the cut bar on the passenger car's side. Surely now their only chance of getting out of this alive, the long steel lever would raise the coupling pin and unhitch the two wagons, thereby ditching the cargo and giving the Cannonball at least a fighting chance of pulling Jess and Sally to safety aboard the rolling stock that remained.

Locking one hand tight around the bar's broad metal shaft, Jess drew in a deep breath, stiffened her every sinew, and hauled hard.

Nothing. The cut bar didn't move. Not a hair.

"Sal! Help me!" Jess yelled, and swinging up, Sally clamped a hand of her own alongside Jess's on the horizontal steel bar. Together, suspended there like rabbits in a butcher's shop, Jess and Sal heaved for a second time, the two wagons they were caught between pitching and rocking, the peak of the parasite mountain now mere centimeters from their air-pedaling feet.

But still nothing. Apparently twisted beyond all function, the cut bar simply would not budge.

And that was when Jess felt the first of the worm things slither around her dangling foot. Choking back another scream, she looked down again and saw a second creature coil its way around Sally's left ankle. "Oh god," Jess blurted, "Sally—"

But then, even as the worm creature attacking Jess squirmed up over her kneecap, the trillopax gave its biggest lurch yet, the two wagons seemed to twist in opposite directions, and all at once the cut bar shifted. With a rusty scrape then a grating squeal, the locking pin jerked free of its hole, the coupler's fat steel knuckle clanged open—

—and the passenger car Jess and Sal hung from flew forward, the pair of them barely maintaining a hold as the crushed remains of the uncoupled freight truck vanished into the dark with the rest of the cargo, while the carriage Jess and Sally clung to hurtled off in the opposite direction.

• • •

Even over the thunder of the Cannonball's engine, Dave heard the roar of the crowd. Heard it as, with a bone-rattling jolt, the loco surged forward, drive-wheels biting into the sand-strewn rails, smoke and steam billowing in vast clouds of black and gray.

Shooting a look behind him through a side window, Dave couldn't help but grin, his heart leaping with relief as he saw the winch wagon cable start to pull free of the thrashing trillopax. Beside him in the cab, Declan let out a whoop of triumph that merged with the hollers of the cheering throng outside, and from the corner of one eye, Dave saw even Sara punch the air.

• • •

Tumbling through the rear end door of the passenger car, then on into the half-crushed carriage itself, Jess and Sally went sprawling across the mangled ceiling—still below them in this upended world—and had barely managed to tear the two attacking worm creatures from their legs when the car's continued pitching sent them both reeling again, this time in opposite directions. At some point during the jolting, rattling chaos that followed, Jess found herself hurled into the space beneath two table seats, and seizing the opportunity, she braced all four of her limbs against the table's sturdy steel pillars, clamping herself in as tight as she could.

• • •

"Oh god oh god oh god oh god," Vera yelled in the upside-down chaos of the lurching crew car, clinging in terror to Isaac as the pair of them watched slick walls of intestinal muscle rush by outside the carriage's broken windows.

•••

And still the Cannonball surged forward, Dave's spirits surging with it, his grin broadening with every meter the loco gained.

Glancing behind him, he saw the trillopax squirm its way upright again, back onto its endless rows of scrabbling legs, then just moments later, the creature's jaws stretched wide, and the front end of the diesel locomotive appeared between those insanely massive teeth. Fewer than ten seconds after that, once the Cannonball had battled its way forward another twenty or so meters, the diesel was free entirely and came crashing down next to the track, canting over onto its side even as the first piece of rolling stock it was coupled to—a crew car, by the looks of it— followed the loco out of the trillopax's gaping mouth. A passenger carriage came next, both it and the crew car slamming down behind the diesel and sending Dave's already sky-high spirits soaring higher still. *So far so frickin awesome,* he thought.

But maybe he should have known better. Because then—

"What the hell?" Declan yelled. "Stop the train! Now!"

Dave slammed the throttle closed, Declan yanked the brake, and seconds later the Cannonball Express came clattering to a halt.

Behind the loco, on the far end of a near forty meter length of taught titanium cable, Dave could see the diesel engine and the two carriages they'd just extracted from the trillopax, all three lying crushed and twisted next to the track.

But that was it.

That was *all*.

Of the eleven cargo trucks that *should* have followed—the very first of which Jess and Sally had been trapped inside—there was no sign.

Dave and Declan leapt from the Cannonball, racing for the wrecked train behind, and as Dave ran, he registered two things: the first was that the trillopax, a gargantuan thrashing nightmare not ten seconds ago, seemed to be sinking once again into the easy slumber of the overfed; while the second was two entirely unmistakable figures—Vera and Lovelight—dragging themselves from one of the crew car's smashed windows and slumping into a heap on the trackside gravel.

"Vera!" Dave yelled as he stumbled up to her and the vet. "Oh god, Vera, are you okay?"

Pulling back the mask of her hazmat—which, unlike Lovelight's, seemed to have survived more or less intact—Vera nodded, though her eyes remained wide with fear. "Sally and Jess!" she blurted. "Are they——" and then those same eyes flashed wider still as they locked onto something else—something farther down the track. "Jess!" Vera yelled, hauling herself to her feet.

Because yes, there Jess was, clambering from a shattered window in the canted passenger carriage behind. Once again, Dave's heart vaulted with relief, his grin rallying.

Staggering the rest of the way to the passenger car, Vera threw both arms around Jess, crushing the bedraggled figure to her breast even as Dave and Declan pulled up behind the pair. "Oh thank god!" Vera said. "Where's Sally? Is she——"

"It's okay," Jess gasped. "Sally's okay," and turning to the passenger car, Jess yelled through the nearest of its broken windows, "Sal! Get yourself out here, gal!"

Still buzzing with the crazy adrenalin rush of it all, Dave maxed out his grin and waited, fully expecting some kind of foul-mouthed Sally-ism to come zinging from one of the passenger car's smashed windows. Everyone else doubtless expected the same, so when all that met Jess's call was a deathly silence, the chill that fell on the group could not have been icier.

Jess frowned, peered into the passenger car's nearest window, tried again: "Sally!"

Still no answer.

Frown deepening, Jess hoisted herself up onto the car's side then leapt back into it through the empty window frame. Dave, Vera, and Declan were right behind her, and for what felt like an eternity, all four of their voices rang out the length and breadth of the wrecked passenger carriage—"Sally! Sal! Sally, where are you?"—their cries growing more frantic with every repetition, more desperate with every piece of debris they hauled aside to look beneath.

But in the end there was only one conclusion to be drawn, and Jess's horrorstricken eyes expressed it fully as she turned to the ashen-faced group and just shook her head.

Sally wasn't there.

She hadn't made it.

21

A Mathematical Certainty

Barely able to draw breath, a tsunami of emotion dammed up somewhere between her breastbone and her choked throat, Vera Middleton hauled herself from the passenger car, pulled down the mask of her hazmat suit, and began to stride towards the trillopax. With every step her world shrank, pulling itself into sharper and sharper focus, her perception narrowing until there were only three things of any importance at all:

There was Sally Chu. Brave, luminous, do-anything-for-a-gal Sally Chu.

There was the monstrous sleeping creature, somewhere inside of which Sally was not—

absolutely *not*—lying dead.

And there was Vera herself. Now the only one in a functioning hazmat. Now the only one who might conceivably be able to rescue Sally.

Three things of any importance at all.

Oh, Vera could *sort of* hear the others behind her, leaping from the passenger car too, their frantic voices thrashing out some kind of desperate rescue plan. But whatever they came up with, Vera already knew it to be an irrelevance. Because in reality there was only *one* viable plan: No matter the danger, no matter what anyone said to the contrary, it was up to Vera. And if any of them tried to stop her, well then, she would jolly well just have to—

"Vera!"

It was Jess's voice.

Vera ignored it and strode on.

"Vera, stop!"

But still Vera marched for the trillopax, the tooth gap she would once again enter by now just meters away. "We have to get her out of there," Vera yelled in answer to Jess, resisting the impulse to turn and look back at her friend. "We *have* to, that's all." And there it was again, that titanic upswell of emotion, the pressure of it building and building, threatening to shatter Vera's every word into blubbering incoherence before it even left her mouth. "We just *have* to," she managed one final time, before stepping up onto the threshold of the tooth gap.

"I *know*," came Jess's reply, and there was such profound understanding in those two brief syllables that Vera *did* pause this time. Pause and then turn to face her friends behind her.

Jess and Declan were both standing by the front of the wrecked diesel, while Dave, boots pounding gravel, seemed to be heading for the Cannonball.

As Vera stood there in the trillopax's tooth gap, barely holding her focus, battling the twin imperatives of tears and trembling, Jess unhitched the winch wagon cable from the front of the diesel and raised its hooked end so that Vera could see it:

"To get you out again. Fast."

Vera opened her mouth to voice some knee-jerk objection... but then closed it again.

Because yes, it made sense. *Good* sense.

In the end, it could even *save* her and Sally's lives...

"Vera, *please*," Jess urged. "It might be your only chance. *Sally's* only chance."

Nodding her agreement, Vera turned and raced back, Jess and Declan setting off simultaneously from the diesel and meeting her halfway. But even as Jess clipped the cable's end to the rear of Vera's harness, Sara Winchester came rushing up.

"Ms. Flint, *stop*," the woman said. "We have a problem."

Jess tugged at the winch wagon cable, testing the security of its fastening to the back of Vera's harness. "Yes, we do," Jess said to Sara. "And we're on it."

"No. I mean the *ore,*" the mining boss insisted. "It's still inside the creature."

"I know. We uncoupled the cargo," Jess explained. "We had no option. It was either the ore shipment or us," at which point, over Jess's shoulder, Vera spotted Dave again, the lad now leaping from the Cannonball's cab and hurrying back to them, some object that Vera couldn't quite identify clutched tight in his hands.

"NO!" Sara barked. "You *have* to listen to me. *All* of you," and this time something in Sara's voice—a kind of barely contained terror—snatched the attention of the group like a gunshot in a library. All eyes on her at last, Sara continued:

"A trillopax is basically a biological fission reactor. Its metabolic system enriches then compresses naturally occurring uranium ore, producing the energy the creature needs to live. Except the ore that *our* trillopax is currently metabolizing is a thousand times more refined than anything found in nature," with which ominous statement Sara gestured to the creature itself, the animal's rear half now giving off a perceptible glow, the clouds of steam rising from its segmented body surging higher than ever. Even through the thickness of her hazmat suit, Vera could feel the heat boiling from the monster.

"Meaning?" Jess said at last, and Sara Winchester's face darkened still further:

"The numbers do not lie, Ms. Flint. *Cannot* lie. That volume of refined ore, at that concentration? Critical mass is now a mathematical certainty."

"Critical…?" Jess actually recoiled a step. "You're not saying…"

"I am," Sara replied. "In fifteen minutes, maybe less, that thing is going nuclear."

22

The Wisdom of Cole Porter

Jess was the one who finally broke the stunned silence. Though still barely able to believe what she'd just heard, she drew herself up, reassessed the scene around her—the glowing trillopax, the gaping crowds, the collective terror of her friends—then turned back to Sara:

"What can we do?"

"We need to get the trillopax out of here," Sara said. "*Right now!*"

But before Jess could respond, Vera thrust herself in front of Sara. "We *need* to save Sally!"

"This entire settlement will be vaporized!" Sara said. "Hundreds will die!"

"*Sally* will die!" Vera pleaded.

"Enough!" Jess snapped. "We can do both," and whirling to Dave, she grabbed the object he'd just retrieved from the Cannonball, shoving it into Vera's hands. "Go!"

Vera took just a second to register what Jess had given her, then nodded and raced off, the winch wagon cable she was attached to unspooling behind her as she sprinted for the trillopax.

"Okay, people," Jess said and began to pace, her head down, her heart pounding, "ideas."

"Can we tow it away?" Declan suggested, his narrowed eyes darting to the Cannonball.

"Not a chance. Too big."

"Lure it?" Dave offered.

Jess shook her head. "With *what?* Not like the frickin thing's hungry. God-*dammit,* what the hell can we do in just *fifteen minutes?*" at which point despair might have claimed Jess completely— claimed the entire group—if not for one person.

All but forgotten since he'd come slumping out of the passenger car with Vera, Isaac Lovelight stepped back into the fray, stumbling up in his tattered hazmat suit, a gleam in his bespectacled eyes. "Excuse me," he said, "but I think I have an idea…"

●●●

Easing herself through the gap left by the

166

creature's missing tooth, Vera stepped again into the rank, deadening darkness of the trillopax, the twin beams from her hazmat's gas lamps blazing out ahead of her to illuminate the glistening, fleshy interior of the sleeping monster.

"Sally!" Vera called, her voice a strident shriek in the near silence. "Sally, can you hear me!"

But there was no response. At least, none from Sally. Just the thick liquid rush of a thousand worm parasites slithering up to Vera en masse and stopping as before at the boots of her hazmat suit. Heart slamming, every breath a gasp of terror, Vera forced her objecting feet onwards, dragging herself and the winch wagon cable deeper still into the acid-dripping gloom of the trillopax's gut, her voice ringing out through the darkness:

"Sally! Sally, are you there! Sally..."

•••

By now, Dave knew exactly what Isaac Lovelight had in mind, and frankly, the idea seemed absurd. Looking on with deepest skepticism as the little vet pulled items from his black leather bag—a bottle of clear liquid, an empty glass flask, some kind of scraper implement—Dave nevertheless kept his mouth shut. The last thing anyone needed here was negativity, no matter the insanity of the course they had chosen to pursue.

Huddled by the trillopax's steaming flank,

Lovelight placed the three items from his bag onto the ground before him, then picked up both the flask and the scraper tool and began to scratch off small flakes from the trillopax's hide, letting them fall into the empty flask.

"Okay, look," Dave blurted, "are you *sure* this is gonna work?"

With a layer of trillopax skin flakes covering the bottom of the flask, Lovelight ditched the scraper, grabbed the bottle he'd taken from his vet's bag, and decanted the entirety of its clear liquid contents into the flask. This done, he tossed the bottle aside, shook up the mixture of liquid and skin flakes, then finally answered Dave's question:

"Oh, my love," he said, "this is a Hail Mary to end all Hail Marys. Almost certainly doomed to failure."

"..." was, in essence, Dave's slack-jawed response. Or possibly, "???"

"*But,*" Lovelight continued, "since luring our friend here with food is a patent non-starter, it *would* seem at least to be a credible alternative, yes? After all, as Cole Porter so wisely points out, even educated flees do it," and with that, Isaac Lovelight turned away, setting off up the track for the winch wagon. Eventually, Dave followed, but not before he'd cast a last doubtful glance at the discarded bottle, still lying where Lovelight had dropped it. The big, now *empty* bottle of Universal

Pheromone Substitute.

•••

Checking the Cannonball's gauges one more time, Jess ticked off the final item on her mental prep list, then stuck her head out a window. Beside her in the cab, Declan slammed the door of the loco's firebox and joined Jess at the same window, the pair of them scrutinizing the scene to their rear.

Beyond the Cannonball's first four trucks—coal tender, crew car, passenger car, flatbed—Jess could see the winch wagon hitched at the very end of the train, along with the slight figure of Isaac Lovelight, just coming to a stop beside it. Moments later, Dave appeared too, stepping past the vet to hop up onto the winch wagon's bed and settle himself in by the controls of the motorized reel mount, the reel itself continuing to unspool titanium cable into the dormant monster behind.

And once again, Jess's thoughts were yanked back to the person on the *end* of that cable—five foot nothing of delicate, pale-skinned, British accountant, heading off alone into unspeakable hell in an effort to find somebody... oh god... somebody who was probably already...

Forcing back dark waves of despair, Jess grabbed the extendible mouthpiece of the cab's voice-tube and barked into it, "Dave? You with me? Is that guy *sure* this is gonna work?"

Jess watched Dave turn to the voice-tube on the winch wagon then lean in to speak, but the reply that emerged at Jess's end was far from the rallying cry of hope she needed to hear:

"Don't ask," Dave said.

●●●

With his mouth pressed to the winch wagon's voice-tube, Dave was on the verge of repeating Lovelight's entire 'Hail Mary' response verbatim to Jess when the vet himself, still trackside with the flask of genetically encoded UPS, leaned in to offer a reply of his own:

"Eyes on the prize, Ms. Flint," Lovelight said. "*You* just be ready to work that throttle," with which words the guy emptied the contents of the flask all over the winch wagon's rear end. "Exactly how frisky our friend here might be," Lovelight continued into the voice-tube, "I have no earthly idea. In all honesty, yes, it's a long shot. It might not work at all, even if we——"

But the man never finished, because just then, with a single monstrous roar, the trillopax emerged from its slumber. Like some kind of colossal insect god-being, the creature reared up where it lay, its front half soaring maybe thirty meters into the air, throwing the entire train into shadow for several seconds, before slamming to earth again with a sound like a bomb blast. Martian dirt rose in vast churning plumes, and then the monster was surging forward through the dust storm, accelerating for the winch wagon ahead.

"Oh my lordy," Isaac Lovelight hollered into the voice-tube, "go go GO!"

23

No Ordinary Loco

No ordinary loco could have done it, Jess knew. Could have achieved the standing start and rapid acceleration needed to stay ahead of the titanic creature barreling at them along the rails behind. But the Cannonball Express was no ordinary loco, and as Jess's hands flew through the last of the complex start-up sequence—releasing the brake, working the throttle, the steam cocks, a dozen more valves and levers—the alien control panel beside her blazed a dazzling green, and the engine gave a roar almost as loud as the monstrous animal heading their way.

Eight heart-stopping seconds later, just before

the advancing trillopax was upon them, the Cannonball's systems loosed a final ear-shattering blast of steam and the loco surged forward. It was the hastiest, most reckless of starts—one that, by rights, should have had the drive-wheels spinning uselessly in place, friction melting the rails beneath—but as ever, the engine's alien-tech-enhancements worked their magic, and the accelerative lurch sent Jess and Declan stumbling backwards, almost tossing them out onto the track behind via the cab's open rear.

Dragging herself forward to the throttle again, Jess risked a glance over one shoulder and could only gasp at the terrifying spectacle of it all: the mountainous horror that was the trillopax, throwing up huge clouds of dust as it raced along in the Cannonball's wake; the vast steamy heat haze shimmering above the creature's glowing rear half; and the crowds, watching open-mouthed as train and monster hurtled out of the mining company's yard, on into the rocky red landscape of the Martian frontier.

●●●

Vera had barely recovered from the trillopax's first unexpected movement—a brutal vertical buck that had sent her rebounding off a fleshy ceiling nearly ten meters above—and was just wishing she knew what was going on outside when she was thrown again. This time the movement sent her staggering horizontally, tumbling over ridges of heaving gut flesh as the creature, apparently awake once more, seemed to surge forward at speed, as if in pursuit of something. And with the signature sounds of the Cannonball Express drifting Vera's way from the creature's head end, it wasn't hard to work out what that *something* might be.

Pulling herself out of the soft mound of muscle into which she'd been tossed, Vera drew in a shaking breath and began again to stumble forward, forcing her way on through the waves of blinding heat now billowing up from the deeper regions of the trillopax's gut.

"SALLY!" Vera yelled. "SALLY, ARE YOU THERE! SALLY!"

•••

Wedged tight between the cable spool housing and the low steel sides of the winch wagon, Dave had no more screams left to stifle, his entire body simultaneously numb with terror and poised to explode into purposeful action when the time came (*if* the time came, the anti-Warwick in him quibbled). Right now though, there was nothing he could do except stay in position and wait. Wait as the Cannonball thundered onward, the trillopax behind it edging closer with every passing second,

174

the winch wagon's spool still dealing out meter after meter of cable into that gaping maw.

"Dave, how we doing back there?" It was Jess's voice, thin and metallic on the voice-tube but clear nonetheless. "The trillopax," she said, "I can't judge the distance too well from here. Is it—"

"—too bloody close!" Dave screamed as the creature summoned an unexpected burst of speed, closing by several meters at once the already minimal distance between its monstrous head and the wagon Dave huddled in. "Oh god, *way* too close! Foot down, Jess—"

● ● ●

"—Foot *right* down!"

The terror in Dave's words—small and tinny though they were over the voice-tube—sent Jess's heart lurching, and with a length of straight track just coming into view up ahead, she rammed her fist into a button on the alien control panel, then opened the throttle still further.

This time Jess was ready for it, bracing herself against some pipework, but once again, the Cannonball's response caught Declan by surprise, the Irishman dropping his fireman's shovel and stumbling backwards as the loco surged with yet more acceleration—uranium mine, township, gawping crowds, all receding into the distance behind as the train hurtled on into the bleak

Martian badlands.

●●●

Through the parasite-infested darkness of the trillopax's gut, fighting even just to stay upright in the pitching chaos and the blistering heat, Vera struggled onwards, her hazmat mask's lamps barely lighting the way ahead at all now as ever denser clouds of steam rolled up from the deeper, overheating regions of the creature's anatomy.

"SALLY!" Vera yelled again, sweat streaming from every pore, her voice growing drier, hoarser, *weaker* with every cry. "SALLY, CAN YOU HEAR ME? SA—"

And that was when she saw it.

Saw it on the listing, heaving floor of flesh ahead of her.

Because while a nearly uniform profusion of worm parasites continued to surround Vera at the level of her feet, up ahead was something that broke that uniformity—an entirely separate and conspicuously dense concentration of the same creatures, squirming and swarming over and under each other in a bulging mound about two meters by one.

Even as she took in that first view of it, Vera swayed where she stood, a black vacuum of despair all but sucking away the last of her already wavering consciousness.

176

And when her eyes finally caught sight of what lay *beside* that wriggling mound of horror, Vera sagged to her knees, her gloved hands trembling as they reached out and picked it up.

Picked up the single torn scrap of shiny black satin.

"Oh god," Vera breathed. "Oh god, no! No no no no NO..."

24

Extraction Plan

In the end, it was a sound that did it. That penetrated the darkness into which Vera, knee-capped by despair, had fallen.

Not that the sound itself was immediately identifiable, just a kind of muffled banging, repetitive, insistent, vaguely metallic, but closer—*much* closer—than the dull clatter of the Cannonball that continued to find its way to Vera from the trillopax's head end.

In fact, it was the very *closeness* of the sound that finally dragged Vera's deadened mind back out of the black and sent her startled gaze darting to the apparent source of the mystery noise; to the mound of writing worm parasites she knelt beside.

Because was this banging sound something that could conceivably have been made by the parasites themselves?

No. Not a chance.

With a gasp that drew in searing, shocking lungfuls of superheated air, Vera plunged two gloved hands into the squirming mass before her, the worm creatures she touched withdrawing at speed to reveal beneath them what may well have been the very last thing Vera expected to find.

It was a door.

A rusting and dented metal door. Leftovers, it would seem, from the part of the train recently extracted from the trillopax; presumably ripped off at the hinges as the carriage it belonged to had been hauled from the creature's gut less than five minutes ago.

Heart pounding still harder, Vera slid her hands to the *other* end of the battered metal panel, the retreat of the worm creatures *there* exposing something else now too: the door's small, cracked window. And behind that window…

Oh god, behind that window a single, blood-spattered, but oh-so-very-*alive* face!

Squeezed beneath the detached door in a shallow fold of muscle, somehow pulling the thick steel rectangle tight against the surrounding gut flesh to keep the worm parasites out, Sally gawped up at Vera through steamy, slime-smeared glass, her eyes widening in disbelief.

"Sally!" Vera blurted. "Oh my goodness, Sally…"

Behind the window, Sally's mouth opened and closed, but with the clatterings of the Cannonball still filling the scorched and steam-filled air, her words were inaudible, and Vera, after shaking her head to indicate this, drew back a little, realizing what she would have to do.

First, she showed Sally the titanium cable—hooked to the rear of Vera's harness and stretching back up through the mists of the trillopax's gut. Then, she extracted from a pocket the object Dave had brought her from the Cannonball's cab, raising the thing to the window of the door so that Sally could see it. Sally nodded at once, the plan—half-assed and all but suicidal though it surely was—apparently clear to her.

Returning a final confirmatory nod of her own, Vera hauled in one last fortifying breath and then reached for the door's recessed handle. "On three!" she yelled, hoping that if Sally couldn't hear her she could at least lip read. "One! Two! THREE!" and together—Vera pulling from above, Sally pushing from below—the pair of them sent the heavy steel door sailing across the width of the fleshy passageway.

The worm parasites were on Sally in an instant, swarming up over her bare skin as the gal threw herself from her hiding-place and slammed into Vera, chest to chest, the force of it expelling every drop of air from Vera's lungs. Straightaway, Sally's legs locked tight around Vera's hips, her left arm around Vera's neck, and using her remaining hand, Sally snatched the object Vera held out for her, taking aim with it over Vera's left shoulder. Even as worm creatures surged up past her neck, cocooning her bloodstained face, Sally pulled the trigger on the oversized pistol and sent a dazzling flash of red rocketing up the trillopax's digestive tract, smoke streaming from the emergency signal flare in a fat, churning contrail.

• • •

Still clinging in terror to the winch wagon of the speeding Cannonball, Dave thought at first that he'd imagined it—imagined that brief flash of red, somewhere in the darkness behind the missing tooth of the creature pursuing them.

But then a moment later, he saw something else. And this time there could be no doubt.

Smoke! Red smoke! Billowing from the monster's mouth!

The signal!

Leaping to his feet, Dave lunged for the floor-mounted gear lever beside him, locked both hands tight around its rubberized grip, and wrenched. With a grind of cogs, the lever shifted in its slot, clunked over into the retract position, and the wagon's motorized spool spun immediately into a full hard-reverse, taking up the cable slack between winch wagon and trillopax.

•••

For several heart-stopping seconds nothing happened, nothing at all, and Vera felt the black close in once more, certain that it was all over; that ahead of her now lay only a horrific and agonizing death with Sally. Sally, who, in the end, would never get to know Vera's true feelings. Sally, who would only ever think that—

And then it came, and the sheer wrenching violence of it was beyond all expectation. Vera gasped in shock, her harness biting hard into her torso as she and Sally—now lost beneath the layers of squirming horror that smothered her—were yanked backwards up the length of the trillopax's steam-filled gut.

As Sally's arms and legs clamped tighter still around Vera's body, Vera held on to Sally in return, and clinging together, the pair of them went careering up the monster's digestive tract, thudding over its fleshy ridges, ricocheting off its muscular walls, dragged backwards at bone-breaking speed by the retracting winch cable.

At some point during the jolting, jarring madness of it, a harsh ripping noise cut through the rumbles of the Cannonball outside, and all at once the lower half of Vera's hazmat suit wasn't there anymore, torn off on some thorny anatomical protrusion they'd struck while flying past. The other half of Vera's suit—mask, gloves and all—followed just seconds later, stripped away in one from right beneath her leather body harness.

Something similar was happening to Sally too, Vera could see, though in *her* case, it was the worm parasites that took the brunt, whole clumps of the attacking creatures shaken free by the relentless impacts, or hooked away on spiky outgrowths of cartilage as Vera and Sally went tumbling on up the dark corridor of the trillopax's gut.

Screaming in pain with every thud and ricochet, Vera threw glance after desperate glance over her shoulder, praying for a sign—*any* sign—that their lunatic ordeal might soon be over.

And at last, she saw it.

Daylight.

Daylight in the shape of a giant (missing) tooth.

A heartbeat later, she and Sally bounced over the creature's gumline, cannoned out into eye-scorching sunshine, and slammed into the dropped tailgate of the winch wagon ahead.

25

Train vs Trillopax

If some forward-thinking genius (Dave, she would later learn) hadn't sought to cushion the edge of the winch wagon's rear with a mass of blankets and matting, as well as halt the winch motor several seconds *before* the literal crunch moment, Vera was pretty sure she'd have ended up permanently crippled from the impact. Even as it was, the jolt to her spine was beyond excruciating—enough almost to knock her out from the pain. But then, through the haze of her semi-consciousness, she felt hands—Dave's hands—hook beneath her armpits, finally dragging both her and Sally safely up onto the bed of the speeding winch wagon.

As Dave set about unclipping her from the titanium cable, Vera, still dazed and groaning, struggled to her feet on the wagon's shuddering platform, while beside her, Sally, now parasite-free, quickly found her own way to upright again.

Which was when Vera became aware of something rather odd: of Sally just standing there staring at her, eyes wide, mouth agape, a picture of dumbstruck disbelief.

And despite the out-and-out insanity that continued to rage all around them—Mars flashing by at record-smashing speeds; unfeasibly gigantic monster on their tail—Vera somehow managed to blush. Yes, *blush*. From the rush of heat to her cheeks, it was surely the full shebang too: traffic light red, jawline to hair roots. She even found herself opening her mouth as if to offer some kind of entirely non-sensical apology for her recent actions, but was interrupted when the trillopax behind them gave a sudden ear-shattering roar and surged forward—closing in, and closing in *fast*.

"Come on, we gotta move!" Dave yelled at Vera and Sally, before whirling to the voice-tube beside him. "Jess, Declan, hold tight, we're on our way!" and spinning as one, the three of them took off for the other end of the winch wagon, leaping across onto the empty flatbed it was hitched to, then racing for the passenger car beyond that.

●●●

Even before her eyes darted again to the clock above the Cannonball's throttle, Jess knew the dark and unwelcome message the timepiece would deliver: Sara Winchester's estimated fifteen minutes were up; their window had closed, and the creature thundering along in the Cannonball's wake could blow any second, sending them all to nuclear oblivion. A further glance to the track behind only confirmed matters, the fearsome orange glow coming from the rear half of the trillopax, and the ever-more-vast clouds of steam it continued to send skyward, telling an illustrated version of the same grim story.

Hauling her head back in the cab, Jess snatched up the voice-tube's handset and barked into it, "Declan, you there? Where the hell are they? Dave *said* they were on their way!"

●●●

Declan could hear the throttled terror in Jess's voice and wished he had something better to tell her. "Sorry, still not seeing them," he yelled into the voice-tube, before turning again to stare out from the rear ledge of the speeding crew car. No matter how hard he peered into the end windows of the passenger car behind though, there was still no sign. "Look, if the guy said they're on their way, they surely can't be— Wait! Yes! YES! There they are!" and despite his best efforts to remain mission-calm, Declan's heart leapt as, only just visible on the far side of the passenger car, Dave, Vera, and Sally tumbled through the end door there and went hurtling up the car's central aisle. In seconds, the trio had covered the length of the carriage and came bursting out the door at its opposite end—the one just across the coupling mechanism from Declan. Half a second more, and all three of them leapt the gap between wagons to join Declan on the rear platform of the crew car.

"Okay, all present and correct!" Declan bellowed to Jess through the voice-tube.

"Then do it!" came her reply. "Now!" and reaching for the grease-caked cluster of engineering between the two wagons, Declan grabbed the coupler's cut bar and hauled hard. With a grind of rusting metal, the heavy steel coupling pin jerked upwards once, twice, then lifted free altogether, and almost immediately, the decoupled passenger car, along with the two cars behind it, began to drift back.

"Clear!" Declan yelled into the voice-tube as the part of the train he and the others remained on—locomotive, coal tender, crew car—began to pull away from the rest.

And not a moment too soon either, because barely had the Cannonball put five meters between the crew car it still pulled and the three unhitched trucks, than the monster on their tail mustered yet another unexpected burst of speed, closing the last of the distance between itself and the winch wagon. With an earth-shaking roar, the trillopax surged up over the three decoupled cars, hauling them off the rails in a titanic eruption of churning dust and billowing steam, and just seconds later, the creature had dragged all three trucks to a complete stop, its massive body coiling around them in a monstrous, twisting embrace.

"Okay, folks," came Jess again over the voice-tube, "you know the drill by now. Time to grab onto something sturdy back there..."

● ● ●

... and at the throttle of the hurtling Cannonball, Jess whirled to the loco's alien-tech control panel, her right hand flying once more to the button array on its glowing overdrive section...

26

Couplings

With a solid CLICK, the overdrive button sank home, the alien-tech control panel blazed its brightest green yet, and Jess locked an arm over the sill of a side window, bracing herself for the Cannonball's response.

It was a response that did *not* disappoint—a neck-jolting, bone-shaking rush of yet more acceleration that flipped the bird to puny physics and rattled reality itself.

At once, in Jess's pounding heart, the Exultation of the Speedfreak crushed the piffling Fear of Death beneath its thundering steel wheels, and gritting her teeth, she gripped the window frame tighter still, urging on her beloved loco: *You can DO this, baby. You can frickin DO this!*

The control panel blazed brighter still; Mars hurtled by outside the cab windows at ever-more-heart-stopping speeds; and behind them, receding at a rate that defied sanity, the trillopax finally mounted the three abandoned wagons in what would surely be its very last act as a living organism. A twinge of unexpected but genuine sorrow for the creature—brain of an earthworm or not—tugged at Jess's heart, and she was just sending on a silent prayer for the poor unknowing animal when a clatter of footsteps cut through the howl of the Cannonball's engine. At the sound, Jess pulled her head back in through the window and turned to see Sally, Vera, Dave, and Declan tumble from the central door of the coal tender, staggering their way up onto the footplate through the cab's open rear.

Relinquishing her grip on the window frame, Jess stumbled forward and threw her arms around Sally and Vera simultaneously, hugging them with a ferocity of emotion that finally trumped what remained of her speedfreak adrenalin rush. "Damn it, gals, but that was too close. *Way* too close."

Hugs (times two) of at least equal ferocity came right back at her, but before anyone could respond in actual words, the trillopax's roar rang out once again from behind, ear-shattering even at the now considerable distance between stationary monster and speeding locomotive.

"Oh man," Sally blurted, "dunno about you lot, but I just *gotta* see this," whereupon the gal in the shredded babydoll abruptly broke free of the three-way embrace and, with what in the circumstances seemed to Jess a rather odd and undue haste, hauled herself up through the cab's roof hatch, her entire ragged, bloodstained, and barely decent self gone in seconds flat.

Hmmmmm, odd and undue haste indeed...

•••

Flopping into the gunner's seat behind the Cannonball's roof-mounted laser cannon, her exposed skin blasted by the air rushing past the hurtling loco, Sally Chu squeezed her eyes shut and cursed her hammering heart. Cursed assorted other parts of her rebellious anatomy too. Group hugs? Yeah, sure, they were all very well, of course they were, but when one of the participants in said hug happened to be someone for whom you had long harbored a lingering fascination (Ha! The Joy of Euphemisms!), and when that very same participant had just recently gone and—okay, let's not fudge the language *here* at least—gone and *saved your goddamn life*... well then, could someone of Sally's healthy and unrestrained passions *really* be expected not to follow through on that hug with a… with a…

Damn, and wouldn't ya just know it, here came the gal herself—in all her tattered yet somehow still immaculate English hotness—following Sally up through the frickin roof hatch why dontcha! Because seriously, what the *hell,* right?

As Vera settled in by Sally's shoulder, Sally considered firing off a quick and casual, "Hey there, gal-pal-o-mine, thanks for saving my life by the way," in hopes that it might at least cover the gratitude side of things for the time being. But somehow, no such dialogue saw its way to emerging from Sally's mutinous mouth, so instead she concocted what she prayed was a smile of non-specific but matey appreciation, following which she hastily returned her gaze to the bizarre monster/train coupling spectacle that continued to unfold in the ever lengthening distance behind the speeding Cannonball.

"Actually, thinking about it," Sally ventured finally, more for the sake of something to say than to voice anything of actual significance, "nuclear blast? Guess we shouldn't really be looking directly at it, right?"

In response to which there came the following unexpected and deeply puzzling reply:

"Meh. So who's looking at *that?*"

—said reply delivered in a *tone* that served only to compound the puzzle; an odd and distinctly *un-*

Vera-like tone that caused Sally to frown in confusion, then turn…

… to find Vera looking straight at her, a kind of nervous-yet-determined smile playing across the English gal's lips.

Sally stood there at a loss. "Um… 'ssup, babe?" she said eventually. "Is something——"

——whereupon Vera threw both arms around Sally's neck, pulled her in with startling force——

——and all at once Vera's lips were there, pressing hard into Sally's while, somewhere in the distance behind, a flash like a million suns lit up the entire universe.

For Sally, the moment was, in every way, a total whiteout—visual, emotional, physical—and when, following that initial flash, a vast billowing mushroom cloud bloomed into the Martian sky behind the hurtling Cannonball, Sally had barely the mental capacity to register it. Even when, infinities later, the apocalyptic *sound* of the blast finally arrived, Sally's faculties were only just beginning to return, the noise of the explosion crescendoing around her like the approving roar of some unseen stadium crowd, the shockwave that accompanied it buffeting her naked flesh like a warm hurricane. And when, at last, with the Cannonball accelerating out of the danger zone, all the sound and fury had died down again… even *then,* was it *Sally* who grasped the reins of this situation? No, it was not. It was *Vera. Vera* who pulled away. *Vera* who dared to make eye contact again. And *Vera,* her slender frame atremble in Sally's arms, who finally offered comment in a single, wonder-filled exhalation:

"Golly," she said.

27

Negotiations

"Please, just take the money," Sara Winchester said, barely pausing to look at either Jess or Declan as she continued to pack the last of her office's contents into a large cardboard box. "Mr. Donovan, I've added ten percent to the price you originally paid for the ore. I hope that's acceptable. And Ms. Flint, you lost a lot of rolling stock because of me. If I've underestimated its value, just let me know, and I'll gladly make up the difference."

Seated with Declan on a pair of battered office chairs, Jess glanced again at the money atop Sara's desk—three separate bundles of the stuff—and, as before, chose to ignore it. Declan did the same.

"You as well, Isaac," Sara continued as she bustled her way past Lovelight, the little vet lurking somewhat awkwardly in a corner. "You do not, I believe, work for free."

But Lovelight too made no move for his share of the cash on the desk.

Regardless of this studied inaction from all three parties, Sara continued with her packing, her eyes darting now and then to Jess and Declan as she went on, "I don't expect either of you to forgive me for what I did, but I always intended to compensate you. *Always.* Please believe that."

Still Jess and Declan said nothing, *did* nothing, and at last their determined non-response got a response of its own, the mining boss turning her frustrations on the silent but conspicuously thoughtful Irishman. "*What?*" she said.

Declan shot Jess a knowing smile, before turning back to Sara. "Okay, listen, I appreciate the gesture, I really do. Losing that ore does kinda delay my people's plans a smidge, but here's the thing... maybe there's a *better* way for you to pay us back."

A frown creased Sara's brow, and she paused, looking Declan up and down for a moment before slumping into her own chair behind the desk.

"The mine here," Declan continued, "it's essentially dead now, right? The entire town in fact."

"Thank you for reminding me," Sara said, her eyes drifting to the room's windows and the view beyond: a yard as bleak and empty as Sara's office now was, the wide-eyed crowds that had gathered in that yard only this morning long gone.

"So what we are left with," Declan said, "is a large workforce, highly experienced in working below ground, none of whom has any love for a local authority that continually screws them on their air tax, and *all* of whom are looking for new jobs. Ideally in a place where their kids can breathe quality air. That about sum things up?"

Jess watched the creases in Sara's brow grow deeper, but before the woman could answer, Declan shifted his attention to Isaac:

"Also, with the entire town here gone, I'm guessing *you* might be finding yourself a little short on work too, huh, Doctor Lovelight? And if such is indeed the case, well, you know… a man of your clearly considerable skills? Could be a real asset to *my* people…"

It was Isaac Lovelight's turn to frown now, he and Sara exchanging looks of deep bewilderment.

"Okay," the mining boss said finally to Declan, "so maybe I should have asked this before but… just who the *hell* do you actually work for?"

Once again, Declan and Jess shared a smile, and then Declan began to talk…

Relieved to be back in overalls, Sally was hard at work in one of the mine yard's rail sidings, bent over the Cannonball's crank pin and slathering grease onto its bearing, when she suddenly became aware of them—of the eyes on her. Pausing in her work, Sally smiled to herself and, while remaining in her legs-astride, ass-to-the-sky position, shot a glance over one shoulder:

"Got yourself a good view there, hon?"

She'd known who it was right away, of course, and who it was blushed as furiously as Sally would have expected in the circumstances, while at the same time pointedly neglecting to retarget those not-so-offending eyes. Instead, Vera Middleton simply smiled through her furious blush and continued to ogle Sally's denim-clad rear. "Oh golly, yes," the English gal said. "Yes I *do*. A *very* good view indeed, thank you ever so much."

Following this choice dialogue, lingering smiles of a rather different quality were exchanged— unspoken promises of what might transpire later when they were all back home—before the moment was broken by a chirpy cockney holler:

"Hey, here she is!" Dave said, hopping down from the Cannonball's cab to wave at Jess as the gal herself (also back in workwear) stepped out of Sara Winchester's office and began to head their way. "Well?" Dave asked as Jess joined the group by the Cannonball. "She gonna go for it?"

Jess nodded. "Sara and Declan will put it to the workers this afternoon, but looking hopeful, yeah. *Very* hopeful."

Sally smiled. "Cool. So I take it that means *we* can get rolling?"

"Yep. Dec's gonna make his own way back to Tranquility later."

"Good to know," Sally said, before wiping down her greasy hands and barking out, "All aboard then, folks! Time's a-wastin'! Or *spit spot,* as our English hottie might say," this last prompting (as indeed it was intended to prompt) a second rose-colored blush from Vera, followed by a flap of faux fury at Sally's shoulder. Delighted with the reaction, Sally grinned and began immediately to herd the gang into the Cannonball.

"Um, sure, okay," Jess said as Sally all but shoved the three of them up into the cab, "we can get going. Any particular reason for the rush?"

Hauling herself into the loco with the others, Sally shot Jess a look of starkest incredulity. "Any particular *reason...* ? Girl, are you frickin *serious?*" and as she yanked the chain above the throttle, the loco's steam-whistle blasted out across the mining compound. "*Date night,* honey! *Remember?* We have got to get *you* plucked, plumped, and packaged."

Jess frowned. "Sally, we've got *six hours.*"

"*Exactly,*" Sally said, her hands dancing over valves, handles, levers, throttle, working their way through the loco's start-up sequence. "Have you *seen* you lately?"

"Nice, Sal. Way to boost a gal's confidence…"

"Oh, honey, fret not. We have *so* got this," and with a hiss of steam, and the gentlest of lurches, the Cannonball Express rolled into motion once more, trundling out of the siding, back onto the Martian mainline. "Because I swear, babe, after ol' Sally has finished with *you* tonight, that boy will be putty in your perfectly manicured hands…"

28

Date Night

"Guess they weren't kidding about keeping a fella waiting, huh?"

Given that Declan's remark had broken a silence (and an awkward one at that) of some considerable duration, Dave Hart was forced to agree. "Guess not," he mumbled, eyeing with reluctance the chiseled and golden-haired Irishman on the sofa beside him. With the soft glow of the oil lamps in the Flint parlor lending said Irishman a kind of romantic Captain America-by-candlelight luminance, Dave (more your Bucky after a bakery binge) stifled a sigh, sank several centimeters deeper into the surrounding sofa cushions, and let the previous awkwardness creep its way back into the proceedings.

Behind Dave, in the cabin's tiny kitchen, Jess's mom, Abby, continued to bustle at the sink, while from an armchair opposite, Jess's little brother, Bill, made his own careful study of Declan, a frown of puzzlement currently furrowing the boy's ten-year-old brow.

"How come you got a date with Jess?" Bill said at last, breaking another lengthy silence.

"Um… because I *like* Jess," Declan answered.

Over by the sink, Abby pursed her lips. "Bill, don't embarrass Declan."

"I like Sally," Bill declared.

"Sally's cool too," Declan agreed.

"*All* the boys like Sally," Bill said, clearly winning some kind of argument in his own mind.

As before, Declan chose discretion: "I guess they probably do at that."

"How come *you* don't like Sally?"

"Bill…" Abby put in.

"It's okay," Declan said to her, before turning once more to the little boy. "Well, as I say, Sally's cool, and really beautiful, of course she is."

"She wears *makeup*," Bill pointed out with evident and gleeful approval. "And fancy dresses and stuff. I've *seen* her when she goes into the Lucky Horseshoe to sing. She's *hot*."

"Ah, yes, but here's the thing," Declan

countered, "there's *loads* of gals out there who *don't* use makeup and *don't* wear fancy clothes, and they *still* look great. Maybe better even than if they did. And, I dunno, I guess that's the kinda gal I've always liked, yes? Gals my grandma used to call a *natural beauty*. Gals like Jess. You see what I'm saying, Bill?"

From where Dave sat, the little boy's skeptical sneer suggested a message not received in any way, shape, or form. Nope, in World of Bill, bustiers and blusher still ruled triumphant.

Over in Daveland, of course, the same message fell on rather more appreciative ears, and even as he dismissed again the possibility of ever being *any* kind of competition for Captain America-by-candlelight, Dave was at least able to enjoy the modest consolation of an opinion shared: Jess Flint, a natural beauty indeed...

●●●

Jess bit her lip and frowned. She just couldn't help it. The person staring back at her from the full-length bedroom mirror certainly caught the eye, there could be no question of that: ebony skin that shimmered with brushed gold highlights; mouth a full and sensual pout of deep red lip gloss; hair an architectural masterpiece of product, styling, and outright Sally magic; and body, filling out one of Ms. Chu's clinging little black numbers with the perfect assemblage of alluring curves. Apparently there were heels to come too. *Heels,* for crying out loud...

In the end, Jess just had to say it: "Sal, are you *sure* about this?"

Reclining on Jess's bed with Vera, the pair of them admiring the fruits of Sally's considerable labors, Sally appeared taken aback. "Huh? Whadaya mean?"

"You look smashing, Jess," Vera said. "Really, you do."

Jess sighed, took another doubtful glance at the stranger in the mirror, absently gnawed off some more of her lip gloss. "Okay, sure, maybe, but is it, you know... *me?*"

Sally snorted. "Oh, girl, please. *Hands. Putty.* You got this."

Before Jess could voice any further concerns, there came a knock at the bedroom door, and after Vera had stepped across to open it, Jess heard Dave's voice from the hallway outside:

"Um, Declan says to remind Jess the film starts at eight."

"Okay, got it," Jess called to the unseen Dave. "But hey, since you're here, a second opinion wouldn't go amiss. What do you think?" and stepping into the doorway so that Dave could see her, Jess proceeded to execute the galaxy's most self-conscious twirl.

As he took in this New Jess, Dave's eyes widened. And not by a little.

Good widened or bad widened though? Jess hadn't a clue.

A momentary silence followed, after which the guy's mouth opened as if about to speak... and then closed again without actually doing so.

But as before, good or bad codfish impression? Who the hell knew?

"Come on, Dave," Jess said. "What do you reckon? Declan gonna like this or what?"

For several seconds more, Dave just stood there, his boyish features betraying a sequence of intense but inscrutable mental workings as he appeared to consider—and consider *very* carefully—what should be his response...

●●●

"Wow! Jess, you look *fantastic!*" Declan said—

—and even from his imperfect vantage point on the sofa in the parlor, Dave was pretty sure he saw Jess breathe a sigh of relief as, standing at the top of the stairs with Sally and Vera, she took in the smiling figure of Declan, gazing up at her from the landing below.

Makeup now all but gone, hair in a pony-tail, and clad simply in smart jeans and her best blouse, a beaming Jess descended the stairs, stepped up to Declan, and gave her date a reciprocal once over, straightening his tie and dusting one shoulder. "Right back atcha, handsome," she said. "So... guess we better get moving, huh?"

While Declan opened the door to the hall, Jess turned to Dave and, after the discreetest of secret smiles, mouthed to him a silent *thank you.*

Dave smiled back, though if he were being entirely honest, it was a smile that *could* have found its way to his lips just a *little* quicker, and one that may also have faltered somewhat when Jess turned again to Declan, linked arms with the guy, and headed out with him into the hall.

"Have a lovely time, you two!" Abby called from the kitchen.

"We will," Jess called back. "Bye..."

And they were gone.

After another moment, the voices of Vera and Sally drifted down to Dave from their positions atop the stairs, Vera opening the dialogue:

"Well then, if I am cooking *you* dinner tonight, I suppose *we* better get a wiggle on. Spit spot!"

"See, *now* you're just *trying* to get me hot..."

There came the faintest of outraged giggles from Vera, then the sound of Jess's bedroom door closing behind the pair as, presumably, they went to repack Sally's tools of the makeover trade.

Alone now in the parlor, Dave did some swift repacking of his own, emotionally speaking, then rose from the sofa and shuffled off to see if he could help Abby and Bill in the kitchen.

● ● ●

Jess and Declan strolled together along the quiet Main Street of Tranquility, the Martian evening dusky and welcoming, the lights of Jolly's Movie House beckoning up ahead.

Well whadaya know, Jess mused as they walked. Dave's tip to dress down for the occasion (not a tip Sally had approved of in *any* way) had clearly been golden. The look on Declan's face as he'd watched Jess descend the stairs was proof beyond question there. Seriously, Jess thought (and not for the first time), could there be a sweeter or more helpful guy than Dave Hart anywhere on Mars? She'd really have to figure out some way to show the fella her appreciation later.

And as for Sally and Vera... well, thank the sweet lord *that* match had finally been recognized by whatever celestial body rubber-stamped these things. About damn time too, in Jess's humble opinion. Several 'rooms' would doubtless need to be 'got' for *that* pair over the weeks ahead, Jess predicted, the thought bringing a smile to her gloss-free lips.

"So..." Declan said as they sauntered on, "good movie this, huh?"

"*The General?* You betcha!"

"Any big names in it?"

"Oh yeah," Jess was happy to confirm. "The Western & Atlantic Number 3. Built by Rogers, Ketchum & Grosvenor, 1855. Twin cylinder, 140psi boiler. A certified classic."

"... Ever think you might need to, you know, broaden your interests sometime?"

Jess looked up at Declan and smiled. "Mister," she said, taking his hand as they ambled down the dusty expanse of Main Street, "I think I just did."

THE END

of

CANNONBALL EXPRESS: *Train Robbers of Mars*

But Jess and her crew return in...

CANNONBALL EXPRESS

Prisoners of Mars

Coming 2021

• • •

WANNA STAY UP TO SPEED
ON THE CANNONBALL EXPRESS?

There are millions of books on Amazon, and we're thrilled you found this one. But if you'd like to know when the *next* CANNONBALL EXPRESS book comes out, instead of leaving it to chance, join the Kit Kane mailing list, and we'll email you on release day.

Yes please! – <u>kitkane.com/join</u>

No thanks, I'll take my chances.

Or to get CANNONBALL EXPRESS updates via your favorite online platform, you can follow Kit on Amazon, Facebook, Goodreads, and others. Use the link below for further details:

kitkane.com/follow

Also, if you've enjoyed this book, please consider leaving an Amazon review or star rating. Big name publishers have millions to spend on advertising, but independently published books like the CANNONBALL EXPRESS series rely largely on reader recommendations. Because of this, an Amazon review (even just a couple of words) or simple star rating can be a massive help.

ABOUT THE AUTHOR

Under a different name, Kit Kane has spent the last twenty years writing comedy, drama, and animation for UK television, contributing scripts to many globally acclaimed series, including Academy Award-winning productions from Aardman Animation and the BBC.

Printed in Great Britain
by Amazon

78558970R00125